ALSO BY NORMAN GREEN

Shooting Dr. Jack

The Angel of Montague Street

Way Past Legal

Dead Cat Bounce

The Last Gig

Sick Like That

Shadow of a Thief

CATCHING THE DEUCE

NORMAN GREEN

Thanks to my friend Raffi from The Bronx, and to D. H. Robbins, for all the support along the way. And thanks to Christine, for everything.

This book is dedicated to all the neighborhood guys who spend their late spring and early summer weekends teaching stray cats how to dream.

APOLOGIA

Sailing ships and buried gold
sail mostly on the screen
banished now to books so old
they're seldom ever seen

but pirates come and pirates go
their time will never end
if you say you don't think so
just get out more, my friend

some things change and some things don't
some fires ever burn
some men learn but some just won't
and catch fire in their turn

so tip your hat in homage now
long may the presses run
truth is that we all learned how
from RL Stephenson

CHAPTER 1

They're not shooting at you, Cheo told himself, but quicker than thought he dodged into an alleyway between two buildings and waited. The whole Bronx seemed to hold its breath along with him, waiting for it to be over. Boom, boom, and then, a string of sharp cracks like fireworks going off, and then, for a moment, silence.

Not yet, he thought, not yet...

Sirens in the distance, the rhythmic howl of an ambulance louder than the rest.

Just a few more minutes.

Cheo Hernandez, a skinny and somewhat undersized thirteen year old Newyorican, lived on the fifth floor of a crumbling brick apartment house on Valentine Street in The Bronx, and getting home safe after school every day was one of his biggest problems. A gang that called itself The Black Hand Crew did business on the northern end of his block, and another gang, The T-Mac Nine, ruled the intersection at the other end. The two gangs ignored one another most of the time because war was bad for business. Business, of course, was crack, horse, vitamin K, eazy E and all the rest of it. Cheo did his best to avoid all that shit, for two reasons. The first reason was his mother. Cheo wasn't sure she was as tough as you needed to be to survive in The Bronx. In fact, in his opinion, she was kind of a fragile soul, and he was sure she would die if he got in trouble. 'There go Cheo, he got busted for fighting and smoking weed, and it killed his moms.'

Forget about it.

The second reason Cheo worked hard to stay out of trouble was a secret. When a seriously good thing falls into your lap you have to protect it, you have to hold it close and keep it safe because if you screw it up, you might never see it again.

He stepped back out of the alley. Two blocks up, where he lived, one of the T-Mac Nine lay face down in the middle of the street. Most of the other gang members were gone, except for a few of The Black Hand crew who looked mesmerized by the ambulance lights. Cop sirens whooped and yowled, getting louder as they drew nearer.

Move it, Cheo told himself, don't stand there looking stupid. He retreated up Valentine, away from the action. Can't walk past The Black Hand Crew, he thought, not now. And you can't go around to the other end of the block, either. The kid lying in the street was probably dead, because the ambulance crew did not seem to be in much of a hurry, and the cops would be there in like thirty seconds. The rest of the T-Mac Nine were probably watching, and you could bet your last nickel the cops would want to talk to you. The problem with that was that then the T-Mac Nine would really, really, really want to know what you said.

No good would come from that. Besides, he didn't need to see. What if he knew the kid? He did not need reminding what The Bronx streets could do to you if you weren't careful.

There was one other way. Cheo hated to use it because it was dark, it smelled bad, and it was creepy. There was a narrow alleyway that ran between two of the buildings one block over from Valentine, it went through a courtyard and under the building right across the street from the one where Cheo and his mother lived. The thing was, one of the supers kept his dog, a muscular, white, mean and nearly hairless beast, tied up in the alley. And the super was even scarier than the dog, and Cheo had no desire to see the guy.

Wait, Cheo told himself. Back up one more block, and wait. Think about baseball…

The Yankees were on a west coast swing, which meant the games were on much later than usual, and Cheo's mother completely did not understand the importance of baseball. The Yankees were playing the Angels and although the Yanks were, in Cheo's considered opinion, by far the better team, that did not seem to deter the Angels from beating on them like the Yanks owed them money or something. Win tonight and they could sneak out of LA with a split… But if Cheo's mother knew he was staying up late to listen to the games, she would freak. Cheo had an old radio with a volume knob that was messed up, if you tried to turn it down so your mother couldn't hear, it would cut out all together. His solution was to stuff pillows and blankets around it to muffle the sound as much as he could.

Two years ago Cheo had heard kids in his school talking about the Little League tryouts over in Parkchester, which was a way nicer neighborhood than his, it was about a dozen blocks east of Valentine. Cheo had tagged along, rode the bus across Tremont Avenue just to see if he could get into a game. He'd had no cleats, no glove, no nothing, just desire, but sometimes desire is enough.

He still couldn't believe he'd done it.

Now, at thirteen he was the starting shortstop and number one pitcher for the Parkchester Cardinals. His favorite person in the world was Derek Jeter. Cheo was darker than Jeter but he liked his hair short like Jeter's and he pretended to be him when he took the field, even though lately he had begun to be troubled by disloyal thoughts. During inter-league play he had seen the Met's shortstop, Jose Reyes, go deep in the hole, field what should have been a clean base hit and then spin completely around and somehow throw out the runner. It was an impossible play, and to make it worse, when Coach caught him practicing the spin move he called it 'hotdogging' and he yelled at Cheo for like an hour.

Cheo had the best hands the league had seen in fifteen years, he knew it because Coach said so when he came to plead with Cheo's mother to let him play. Coach had been there, watching, that first day. There had been no one to tell Cheo how to catch the ball that first day, no one to tell him how to cock the bat. It was not a real game anyway, not even a real practice, just a bunch of kids fooling around while they waited for the rest of the adults to show up. Cheo had been taken next to last when they chose up sides but no one challenged him when he installed himself at short. The rituals of the game unfolded, honored and esteemed no higher anywhere than at that particular time and place. The other team sent a batter up to the plate and a moment later Cheo heard the loud 'pank' of the metal bat as it sent a hard grounder to his left. He could see the laces on the spinning ball, he could almost read the trademark as he slid over and crouched down in the path of the ball, he felt that good sting in the palms of both hands as he caught it, then he took one step and slung the ball to the first baseman. He had a feeling as he let the ball go, an idea that got bigger and stronger as the first baseman stretched, caught the ball and stepped off the bag pumping his fist and yelling at the runner, who was clearly out, and then he was sure of it a second or so later when one of the older kids on the other side walked his own baseball mitt out as far as the pitcher's mound and tossed it to Cheo. "Gimme it back when you got ups," the kid said, and Cheo, nodding agreement, knew. He might still be just one more skinny undersized Puerto Rican kid, just another yellow Lego in a Bronx-sized box of seemingly identical bits, but when he stood on a baseball diamond, everyone on that field would know that he had game. Later, riding the bus home that first afternoon, he felt taller than he ever had before, because for the first time in his life he believed in something. He had faith. He knew there was a place for him.

He was real.

"Mrs. Hernandez, you don't understand." Cheo could still hear Coach's voice, one of the few times he ever heard it without any yelling involved. "Cheo's hands are a gift from God, I swear to you, baseball could be his ticket..."

"He's eleven years old!" his mother had cried. "You want me to let him walk through this neighborhood all by himself, past the drug dealers and the gangs and the *vatos* who hang out down by that park? Look at him! He's so small..." Cheo could hear it in her voice, she wanted him to stay eleven forever, she wanted him to stay locked up in his room until he was about a hundred years old.

"I understand, Mrs. Hernandez, really I do, and I'm not trying to take your little boy away from you. I just want to teach him to play the game the right way. I'm telling you, he was born for this. My brother in law's neighbor is the athletic director at the Sacred Heart Academy and believe me, he is gonna flip when he sees..."

"Mr. Mitchell, I am sorry." Cheo's stomach still turned over when he remembered that moment. "There is no chance that I can afford tuition at a private school..."

"You let me worry about that," Coach told her.

"What are you talking about?"

"They'll find the money. Believe you me, those Salesian Brothers like a winning team just as much as the next guy. Maybe more. When he reaches high school..." And right then the continents had shifted, they must have, because from that moment on the world became sweet, and wonderful. There was, at last, a good reason to put up with all of it, to fight your way through another day.

There was baseball.

Out in L.A, the Yankees were getting spanked, and by a rookie pitcher, no less. Cheo, hoping for a rally but thinking he really should turn off the game and go to sleep, looked out his window. Someone came around the corner, turned off the cross street and started down Valentine. It was a strangely hunched figure, one shoulder up higher than the other, but as the figure limped under a streetlight Cheo could see that it was a White guy, and it wasn't a hump he had on his back but a knapsack. He had dark hair, ratty construction boots and ragged clothes. The Black Hand Crew had a few guys holding the corner but they didn't mess with the guy.

Which was odd.

The guy is either a cop or a bum, Cheo thought. No other White guys on this street, not at this time of night.

A police cruiser turned onto Valentine a moment later but when Cheo looked for the White guy he was gone.

Vanished.

The cop car eased on down the block, neither speeding up nor slowing down. A moment later Cheo noticed something stirring in the shadows and then he was back, knapsack up on his shoulder, limping as before. But limp or not, you had to give it to the guy, he was smooth and

Coach preached smooth all the time, to Coach, smooth was right up there with cleanliness, next to God.

Some of those guys with the Black Hand Crew had been his schoolmates once. They seemed to get a lot of joy out of riding him when he passed by wearing his uniform, carrying his cleats and glove in a plastic Food Town shopping bag slung over his shoulder. 'Yo, Che, why you wastin' your time with that shit? Come with us, my brother, we could use you. We *neeed* you, man...' Cheo never told his mother about it. You kidding? How stupid would that be, go and cop to her that things were even worse than she imagined? That could get your baseball privileges suspended for life. Cheo's secret dream, the one he never told anyone about, was to someday stand on the mound at Yankee Stadium, stare in at the batter while fifty thousand people screamed in his ear. Didn't matter who he played for, either, the only thing that mattered to him was being there.

Throwing the pitch.

"Bring da heet!" His catcher, a Polish kid that everybody called City Island Pete, loved to yell that no matter how many fingers he was holding down or how many times Cheo shook him off. "Bring da heeet!" And Coach would yell at both of them to shut up and play but it didn't matter much, Cheo only had the fastball... On a good day, nobody could touch him. On a bad day, he had to work it. City Island Pete had to ride two busses to get to Parkchester and he took his share of grief on the street behind being the only White kid but he burned to play ball, he could handle a bat, and all the fighting had made him tougher than a two dollar steak.

The guy with the limp paused by the trash cans out on the sidewalk in front of Cheo's building and peered at the numbers on the door. Forgetting the radio for the moment, Cheo eased over to his open window and stuck his head out. A few seconds later a door opened in the alleyway beneath him and yellow light spilled out over the stained concrete. The building super, whom Cheo's mother did not like because he got high, stepped out and embraced the man with the knapsack. "Pelios!" he croaked. "You make it! By God, you make it! Wha' hoppen to your knee?"

"They had a go at me inside," the man rasped. "How about a beer? I haven't had a beer in..."

"Lemme guess," the super said, cackling. "Twelve and one half year. C'mon inside."

The cell block was on lockdown when the corrections officers came for him, the captain and three other guards carrying leg shackles, a belly chain and handcuffs. A murmur rolled through the building like a wave running up the beach, the normal jailhouse noise died away and left an uneasy silence in its wake.

Somewhere, one man started to chant. "Greek. Greek. Greek."

The three guards entered his cell while the the captain waited outside on the tier, hefting his club. "Pelios," the captain said. "You hear that?" The chant was slowly growing louder, gaining momentum. "Your people. The animal chorus."

Pelios, chained up now, shuffled out of the cell, limping on his bad knee. It doesn't mean anything, he told himself. Just another excuse to make a racket. But the chant echoed through the concrete building, low and deep, five hundred male voices chanting: "Greek. Greek. Greek."

The guards took up their positions, one in front of him, one to each side, the captain in back. "Walk," the captain said, and they began their slow march down the tier, Pelios shuffling between them like a wounded bear.

"Tell me something, Greek," the captain said.

Pelios kept moving, eyes on the ground.

"How old are you?"

Pelios did not respond.

"That's all right," the captain said. "I looked it up. You're thirty-four."

"So what," Pelios said, his voice rasping like sandpaper on rock.

"You know something, Pelios? I did the math. You've spent over half your life in prison. And that's not even counting juvie. What's the real number, Greek? How long have you been locked up? Do you even know?"

Pelios shook his head. He didn't like to think about the past. He did his time by staying in the day, moment by moment, by refusing to allow his mind to wander the dark corridors of his history.

By the time they reached the end of the tier it seemed like the whole building was chanting. "Greek! Greek! Greek!" Pelios wondered if any of them felt anything real for him. Envy, maybe. Fear, by some. Rage by more than a few, without question. You did not survive prison without making a few enemies. It would be tough to recognize anything other than hate that might pass for an emotion in this place. But the chant continued to grow.

They turned left onto the metal catwalk that would lead them out. "Whatever," the captain said. "Twelve and a half this time. Twelve and a half years for taking a man's life. For killing a father, a husband, a grandfather. Don't seem fair, does it?"

Pelios flashed on the face of the old man he'd been convicted of killing. Oddly enough, the old man had been the one everyone called 'the Greek' back in the day, and whatever else he'd been, he'd been a hard case right to the bitter end.

"You know what gets me, Greek? You know what really frosts my balls?"

Pelios held his tongue. It was a speech, anyhow, not a conversation.

"You could have walked out of here two years ago. Two whole years! But you wouldn't do it, you declined parole. What kind of a man serves two extra years in prison just to get out of parole? Did you hear the rumors, Pelios? Did you hear what they were saying about you two years ago? Because nobody could find that old man's money after you killed him. They said you had it stashed somewhere. Is that right? You got it hid someplace? But you couldn't get to it, that's what they all said, because that old man's got a son and three or four grandsons and they all want to see you bleed. And that's why you declined parole. Because you were afraid."

Pelios concentrated on his limping progress. There was a locked door in sight, he knew, but he refused to look up at it. Behind that locked door was a long concrete hallway that ended at another locked door which he had last seen twelve long years ago. He could feel his heart thumping in his chest but he gave no outward sign that he felt anything at all.

"I never believed in the talk," the captain said. "I know damn well why you stayed inside. If you'da took parole, you'da got saddled with a parole officer. You'da had to pee in a cup. Stay clean, get a job. Report in twice a week. Answer questions. No drugs, no booze. You can't stand nothing like that, can you, Pelios? You ain't got the constitution for it. Did you know we got a pool running on you? On how long you'll manage to stay out this time. The over/under on you is running right at sixty days. I'm taking the under. I'm betting you won't last a month before you're locked up again."

Pelios kept his hoarse voice flat and unemotional. "You'll never see me again, captain. Not in here."

"Bullshit." The man put some anger into the word. "You can't make it on the outside. That's why we build places like this, Pelios, to keep men like you away from the rest of us. Oh, I know you're a smart guy. Got your GED this time, even got you some college. Honest man such as myself, it ain't bad enough I got to pay to send my little girl to school, but they spend my taxes to send your ass, too. What a goddam waste of money."

"But you know I sure do appreciate it, captain."

"You wanna know why you won't make it on the outside, Pelios?"

"I'm listening," Pelios said.

"Your body might be thirty-four, hell, your liver might be sixty, but up in between those ears where it counts you are still what you always been, you're a thirteen year old grade school reject with an attitude and a gun, and the first man out there that cuts across you or mouths off to you is gonna catch a bullet for his troubles. You don't know what it takes to survive on the outside, and you wouldn't be man enough to pull it off if you did know. You're a predator. You're a user, you don't give a good goddam about anybody but yourself. You ain't man enough to walk free with the rest of us, Pelios. You belong back there inside that cell, and if I had any say you'd never see the light of day again."

"God bless America, captain. I am a new man."

The five of them stopped in front of the first door. The guard in front of Pelios stared up at the camera mounted high on the wall. "One for transport!"

Pelios could hear the man behind him twisting his wooden baton in his hard fists. Not a good sign. Another day, he knew, his mouth would have already earned him a beating. "What's your degree in, Pelios? What did you study?"

"Psychology."

"You gotta be kidding me. Now that's just a goddam shame."

The lock on the door buzzed and the guard in front yanked it open. Pelios shuffled through into the corridor. When the door closed behind them the lock snapped shut and the sounds of the chant died away.

The old man's people, the friends and relatives of the man they'd said he killed, they would be waiting for him. For the first time in twelve and a half years he allowed his mind to range beyond that second door. You live through the first twenty-four hours, he told himself. You get through the first day and you might have a chance.

"Greek!" The captain, apparently, was not finished. "Next time around, only way you get out of here is inside a box."

Pelios, straightening up, ignoring the pain in his knee, shook his head.

"Ain't gonna be no next time," he said.

He felt just like a target in a pinball machine. He stood just outside the gate, blinking in the harsh sunlight, reeling in the unfamiliar sensation of the wind blowing across his face. The corrections department bus waited just across the parking lot, the driver smirking at him through the open door. I get on that bus, Pelios thought, and I'm toast. Too bad I don't have a lot of other choices. Maybe I should just run.

He heard a car engine crank and then cough itself awake. He turned toward the sound, watched a big 70's era Caddy ease slowly across the parking lot in his direction. The driver was a bald White guy with a thin face and sunglasses. The car came to a stop next to Pelios and the passenger side window slid down. "Get in," the guy said. Pelios thought the guy's voice sounded familiar but he couldn't place it. He looked back over at the bus, saw the bus driver, eyes wide, fumbling frantically with a cell phone. The guy driving the Caddy took his shades off and Pelios recognized him from the hawk's eyes set deep in his skull, the pupils that never looked in quite the same direction. He bent down to get a better look.

"Dzekas," he said. "That you?"

"In the flesh," he said. "What's left of it, anyhow. Listen, if I was gonna kill you, you'd already be a dead duck, so relax. If you get on that bus over there, the old man's people will get you. They're waiting for you at the train station."

Pelios got in. He stared at Dzekas as they pulled out of the parking lot. "What happened to you?"

"Cancer," Dzekas said. "Great way to lose weight."

"You gotta be down about a hundred pounds."

"About."

"How bad?" Pelios asked him.

"A year ago they gave me six months."

"Sorry to hear it." Pelios looked over his shoulder. "Nobody following," he said. "But that guy in the bus has got to be giving them this car and the plate number right now."

"He ain't giving them nothing," Dzekas said. "My car's parked about a mile from here. Once we dump this car and get into mine, we're home free." He squinted at Pelios, then put his shades back on. "This ain't my first time at the dance, you know. They ain't nobody catching me."

"Sorry. I didn't mean to question your, um, abilities. But why are you doing this? I figured you'd be working with the old man's son. Vasilios and them. Trying to get me."

"I don't work for nobody. Besides, it's his daughter Tasya you gotta watch. She's meaner and smarter than Vassi ever thought of being. Anyway, as an official, supposed to be dead already person, I'm on borrowed time. You know what that means, Pelios?"

Pelios just watched him.

"It means that now I'm playing with house money. Don't matter what I do. I can't lose." He seemed to think that over for a second or two. "Actually, the only way I lose is if I don't get done the things I need to do before my time runs out."

"Like what?"

"First of all, I wanna put a few things right. Make up for some of the stuff I done."

"You're not serious."

"Serious as death. And you're on my list."

"What did you ever do to me?"

"Way back when the old man took you off the street, he was talking about sending you to school. Letting you grow up regular. I told him I didn't see what good that did for us, we needed smart guys and muscle, we didn't need no Little Leaguers. Or accountants. Or whatever the hell you would'a turned into." He glanced at Pelios. "I coulda made a difference for you, and I didn't do it. Always felt lousy about that."

"And for that I get safe passage."

"Anywhere you want."

"You can drop me in The Bronx."

"Really? What's in The Bronx?"

"Nothing." Pelios looked over at the older man. "Did you really split from the old man's people?"

"Yeah. I'm done with that life."

Pelios considered. "It's the money," he finally said. "It always comes back to that. And everybody knows how often the old man went out to Calvary Cemetery in Queens, to visit his dead mother."

"Yeah."

"Which really means, they know he wasn't going there to visit his dead mother, who he didn't much care about one way or another."

Dzekas nodded his head. "We all figured he was burying his money out there somewhere. Burying it, hiding it, piling it up out there someplace. And since you were his driver, and since nobody else knew where it was..."

"Exactly," Pelios said. "So you see my problem. I can't just go walking in there with a shovel over my shoulder. I got to find out who my friends are, first."

"Money ain't got no friends," Dzekas said. "Tell you the truth, you prolly wouldn't be able to trust me, neither, but being already dead, I don't count."

Pelios was silent for a moment. "I did twelve and a half years for her, Dzekas. I can't believe she doesn't feel something."

"You know what, you never could think right when it came to Tasya Gaitanis."

"So she's using the old man's name now," Pelios said, surprised. "Well, I know what you're gonna tell me."

"That she's Satan's baby sister? I ain't gonna tell you no such thing, because I've told you that before, and so have lots of other people, including her father. You didn't listen then, why would you do it now?"

"That's why I want to go to The Bronx," Pelios said. "I'm staying away from Calvary, and from Astoria, and from her and her brother Vasilios and the rest of them. I'm gonna make them come looking for me. That way I should be able to tell who's on my side and who wants me dead."

"She'll stick you," Dzekas said flatly. "You get the two of you in the same room, add in the money, I can tell you exactly how it'll go down. You get one look at her and you'll go all stupid. She'll stick you with that little knife she carries and she'll leave you dead on the floor, walk right out the door with your dough. Period. End of story."

"Maybe. But I plan on giving her the opportunity to make that choice. Her and Vasilios and the rest. It's the only way I can know for sure."

"I'll pray for you," Dzekas said.

"Yeah, thanks," Pelios said, but then he looked over at Dzekas. "You're serious, aren't you?"

"Serious as death."

"Well, all right, I'll take whatever help I can get. But whose side are you on? Where do you come down in all of this?"

"I ain't on nobody's side. I meant what I said, back in the parking lot. I wanted to square things between you and me while I had the chance. But I ain't gonna lie to you, there's something I need to do before my time comes and I'm a hundred and twenty grand short of getting it done. A trivial sum such as that, I figure there ought to be more than that laying around loose when this is all finished."

"You want to work with me, there'll be more than that. A lot more."

"Don't need more. And I'm serious, man, I'm done with all that. When you get as close to the finish line as I am, your way of seeing things changes."

"For what it's worth, I'm really sorry to hear about..."

"My impending demise?"

"I tell you what. You give me your word that you won't help Tasya or Vasilios, and I'll get you your hundred twenty when this is all over."

Dzekas nodded. "I can't ask for no fairer than that. You have my sacred promise as a liar and a sinner. So what do you do now? How are you gonna entice them to come up to The Bronx to chase you?"

"I'll think of something," Pelios said.

Cheo headed up towards Tremont Avenue to catch the bus, thinking about last night's game. Twice a year, once around Thanksgiving and once more sometime around spring break, Cheo's mother could be counted on to tearfully insist that she and Cheo begin attending church. Cheo did not enjoy it much, he was suspicious of new things, particularly ones that required bathing beforehand, but he was powerless to resist his mother when she cried, he couldn't imagine anything that made a guy feel worse than that, so he went. It was on one of those infrequent forays into the realm of the spirit that he heard the story of Samson, who, according to the preacher, lost his mojo when his girlfriend cut off his braids. Cheo pictured it, a big guy passed out in bed, all hung over and sweaty, his dreads all over the floor... It didn't seem real when he first heard it, it sounded more like something you'd see in a movie. Lately, though, he had begun to suspect that it might be possible, sometimes things that didn't make any sense happened anyhow. And it didn't have to be because of hair, either, maybe it was the water in LA, otherwise how could you explain the Yankees dropping three out of four to a team like the Los Angeles Angels of Anaheim, who couldn't even decide what city they wanted to be named after? You should talk, he silently berated himself. Last time you pitched you did three innings, six hits, one homer, three runs. And he couldn't blame it all on the ump, either, even if the guy did squeeze the zone whenever the little kids came up to bat. Cheo figured the guy liked to see anybody who was small and cute get a hit. He'd managed to repress the urge to suggest the guy give them four strikes instead of three only by reflecting on how lame it would be to get thrown out of the game behind being a smartass. Dude! I'm trying to win a game, here...

The cops had the street in front of him closed off, they had two cars pulled over and there were flashing lights everywhere. It forced Cheo to change his normal route, which made him a little uncomfortable. One block over, he told himself, what's the big deal? But you never knew.

Anyhow, he was almost up to Tremont, and once he got to Tremont he was good. But sure enough, when he turned the next corner there was a bunch of guys halfway down, they were sitting on car hoods and hanging out, they each had a black bandana hanging halfway out of a back pocket. They were part of the Black Hand Crew and he had a feeling they weren't going to let him pass this time without a hassle but he crossed over to the other side of the street and kept going anyhow. Thinking about the homer, which was his fault and why his team lost, made him mad all over again. Half his fault, anyhow, and half because of that stupid umpire. If you're gonna call everything a ball, what's a pitcher supposed to do? But when he grooved one to a tall outfielder named Ramon Something, Ramon had crushed it, hit it halfway to Southern Boulevard, trotted home behind the two pint-sized infielders that the umpire, Mr. Generosity, had put on base ahead of him.

Two of the tallest kids got off a car hood and crossed the street in front of him, a couple more circled around behind. Cheo could feel his breakfast trying to crawl back up out of his stomach but he did not consider running away, at best that was only a beating, deferred. They would either get you now or get you later. What was the difference? The biggest one stood squarely in his path. "Where you think you're going?"

Cheo, well-schooled in the etiquette of The Bronx streets, told him nothing. "No place," he said.

"Choo doing?"

"Nothing."

"How come you all dress up like A-Rod? Huh? Tryina be mini A-Rod?"

His lesser associates all howled at this remarkable display of wit while Cheo considered his reply. There is little mercy on the street, he knew, and certainly no forgiveness of sin. And the sin was his: if he, Cheo, had been more careful, none of this would have happened, but now he was going to have to pay.

Should have gone over one more block, but it was too late for that now.

What could you do?

Might as well get it over with.

"No," he said. "But I didn't want nobody thinking I was a pussy, you know what I mean, going around with my hankie hanging outa my pocket like some kinda mama's boy. Know what I'm saying? Ain't that what they call you guys? The Mama's Boys?"

The big kid took a step in Cheo's direction, his fists coming up, but then he looked at something behind Cheo and his eyes went wide. Out of the corner of his eye Cheo saw one of the kids behind him fly through the air, bounce off a car trunk and land in the street. He turned around in time to see the White guy with the limp rip a black pistol out of another kid's grasp and hit him in the face with it. Blood bloomed out of the kid's nose and he shrieked. Cheo turned front again to see the rest of them running away, all except the ringleader, who, affronted, was a second and a half too late. When he turned to run the White guy was all over him, rode him down to the sidewalk. Almost casually he placed the pistol at Cheo's feet. "Watch that," he rasped, and then he turned his attention to his victim. "Shut up," he said to the tall kid, who had started squalling, and he smacked him hard on the back of the head. "Shut up, shut ya little punk-ass up. What's the name of this street? Do you know the name of this street?"

"This is a hundred and twenty-fourth..."

"No it ain't," the White guy said. "This is my street. You hear me?" Whack. "MY. STREET." Whack. "That means everything on this street belongs to me. Everything in your pocket is mine." Whack. "Your shoes are mine." Whack. "Your ass is mine. You hear me?"

The kid had started sobbing, he was not used to this, he was used to being the big dog. Cheo would have felt sorry for him, except, you know. You can't cry, no matter how scared you are.

You just can't.

The two of them watched the kid scamper down the block. The man with the limp, still down on one knee, looked at Cheo. "Baseball player, huh?"

Cheo looked down at his uniform. "Duh," he said.

"I know," the man said. "Stupid question. What do you play? What's your position?"

"Shortstop," Cheo said. "And pitcher. They gonna come for you. You know that, right? I mean thanks and everything, but you made them look bad, and they got some big guys that run with them. They need to hurt you now, or else they look like losers."

"They are losers. Pitcher, huh? You any good?"

Cheo was surprised. The dude did not seem very smart. White guy in the hood, he ought to be more concerned with his well-being. "Mostly. But they hit me hard last time out."

"Too bad. What do you throw?"

"Fastballs. Coach says I'm too young to learn breaking pitches. Says they'll mess up my shoulder."

"Sounds like a smart man, your coach. You should stay away from hard sliders and all that, but you can learn a big slow curve. Got a ball on you?"

"Yeah." Cheo fished it out. He'd found it last year, down in the weeds at Crotona Park. It was battered and beaten, dirty and ill-used but it was a real baseball, and would do.

"Let's see you pitch," the guy said. "Only don't throw it. Just pretend."

"Okay." Cheo toed the curb just like he'd done a million other times, leaned in and squinted at the catcher for the sign, checked the runner on second, wound up and stepped off into the street while aping his throwing motion. It wasn't the same as throwing from a dirt mound, but it was close enough.

"Lefty," the guy said. "Pretty good. Nice easy motion. Nice long stride. Show me how you hold the ball."

Cheo complied.

"You know what, you got big mitts for a little guy, Lefty. You think those jerks would have messed you up?"

Cheo shrugged. "Mostly they just smack you around. But they gonna be plenty pissed off at you."

"Yeah? Try turning the ball, put your index finger right next to the horseshoe. See how the laces make a horseshoe? Like this." He took Cheo's hand into his own, repositioned the ball in Cheo's fist. Cheo could feel the hard skin on the man's fingers.

Not a wino, then. Not a cop, neither, you didn't get hands like that from hassling people and writing tickets.

"Yeah. That's the grip. The trick is, you got to throw it exactly the same way you throw your fastball. Same exact motion, except you hold the ball like this and you turn your wrist like so, that will give it spin when you let it go. That's what makes it dive. You mess around with it a little bit, you'll get it. What you want is a big slow curve, the kind that goes from twelve to six o'clock. And don't throw it a lot, don't even practice it a lot. Keep it in your pocket, save it for when you really need it."

Cheo nodded, scowling at the baseball, memorizing the feel of it in his hand. "They could shoot you," he said.

"Only if I give them the opportunity. They're just punks, Lefty. If they come looking for trouble, they'll find plenty."

"They ain't gonna let you go." Cheo was sure of it.

"You live around here?"

Cheo nodded. "On Valentine. You?"

"Around the corner," the guy told him. "They'll probably send someone to ask you about me, but I don't think they'll mess with you too much, not until they're know what they're dealing with. You okay with that?"

Cheo shrugged. His future was only speculation, tomorrow might come and it might not.

"When they front you, you tell 'em it was Pelios that rousted them. You tell 'em you're with me now. They mess with you, they gotta deal with me. Can you remember that? Pelios, the Greek."

"Yeah." This guy was either very dumb, or very bad. "You, um, you did this on purpose. You want them to come looking for you."

Pelios grinned. "You stay outa trouble, Lefty."

'Lefty' was the coolest nickname he'd ever heard in his life... "Okay. Thanks. Mr. Pelios."

He played catch with himself as he walked down the block, alternating his grip between his normal one and the new one Pelios had shown him, concentrating on the feel of the ball as it left his hand. At the end of the block he stopped and looked back, but Pelios was gone.

Lefty was about the same age Pelios had been when old man Gaitanis had taken him in. The old man's approach had been crude but effective, just like the man who used it. Sooner you knew that about him, the better… The old man had watched Pelios and three friends throwing rocks at a bread truck on the streets of Astoria, Queens. He'd said nothing at the time, but a few days later he'd presented each of the kids with a watch. It had been a gaudy thing, and cheap, but it had looked flashy and cool to Pelios. A few days later Pelios sported a busted lip and a black eye but he was the only one of the four who'd managed to hold on to his watch.

That had been enough for the old man. "Hey kid," he'd said. "You wanna make some money?"

Offer a street kid money, he's gonna take it. But in a lot of ways it had been the end of the line for Pelios, he would never play in another baseball game. Yeah, he made some money, but it wound up costing him everything he cared about.

Funny how you could only see something like that after it was too late.

I ain't like the old man, Pelios told himself. I won't ruin things for Lefty, I swear to God…

But he couldn't shake the bad feeling that had lodged in the back of his throat.

CHAPTER 2

The team comes first.

That's what they always said about Jeter, they said he was a team guy. Cheo wanted to be a team guy, too, so even when he wasn't wearing the uniform, he was a Parkchester Cardinal. The day was fast approaching, he knew, when he would be too old to play in the league. He hoped that he would go on to play for other teams, high school first, and maybe the minors after that, or a college team, but found it hard to picture himself in those far-off places, couldn't figure what he would look like, didn't know what the names of those future teams might be. Not that it mattered, the names teams gave themselves were pretty dumb. There were no real cubs in Chicago outside of the zoo, no pirates in Pittsburgh, neither, and everybody knew there was no such thing as a devil ray. And who cared what color socks you wore? Of course, he had never seen a real cardinal in Parkchester, nor anywhere else for that matter. A three-legged dog, yeah, sure, there was one in one of the junkyards near the Bruckner Expressway. And how funny would that be? An honest name like that, we're The Parkchester Three-Legged Dogs, if we can catch you we'll bite a big chunk out of your ass...

The Yankees, now there was a noble name, what the hell was a Met anyhow? A theater in Manhattan, where the fat lady sings. But the

Yankees were the first Americans, they got here before anybody except for the Indians, which poor unfortunates wound up in Cleveland, and that had to suck. But the Yankees, the real ones, they built the first cities, made the first roads, they wrote the Constitution, probably. If you were a Yankee, you could be proud of the name.

But Cheo was a Cardinal, he would still be a Cardinal long after they made him give the uniform back, even when he was old and dead, somewhere deep inside he would still be a Parkchester Cardinal, and nothing would ever be cooler than that. Which was why he only threw fifteen curveballs. Okay, at first it was only going to be ten, but not many of those turned out to be curves, a few of them were grounders and two were airballs that City Island Pete had to go chase down, but numbers nine and ten started to look like something, so he chanced five more. Any more than that would have been disloyal, the Cardinals had a game to win and Cheo would be on the mound for three innings.

The team came first.

And on this particular day, everything was different. Cheo's fastball popped City Island Pete's glove with a satisfying crack, and the ball mostly went where he wanted it to. And nobody got a hit, nobody even got any good wood on him, there were a couple of pop-ups and some foul balls but none of them got out of the infield. By the middle of the second inning he had them chasing the outside pitch, and by the time he moved to short the other team was already beaten, Cheo and his teammates were up four-zip, which was how it finished.

Pretty good day to be a Parkchester Cardinal.

Plus, he had the curve now, it was like having a secret girlfriend. He would keep working on it with Pete whenever he got the chance. How sweet was that?

Coach was so happy about the win that he took the whole team to Burger King afterwards. Cheo had been to Burger King a few times before and he loved the way the place smelled, loved the taste of the hot french fries, loved that you could get a big milkshake for after. "You guys were great today," Coach told them. "That was a quality team we played out there, last year those guys went to the borough finals and you guys completely shut them down. I'm proud of all of you." Then he went through the team, position by position, and he told each player what he'd done right and what he'd done that he could do better next time. He saved Cheo, City Island Pete and Arturo, who was the day's other pitcher, for last. "Pete," Coach said. "You're turning into a fine backstop. You gotta get out after those pop-ups a little quicker, though. When you see that ball go straight up, just jump out of your stance, chuck your mask away and go get the ball. And we're gonna get you a little extra B.P. on Saturday. You got some good swings today." Then he turned to Arturo and Cheo. "And you two," he said. "I don't even wanna say what I wanna say about you two because I don't want you getting swelled heads. Just promise me one thing."

Cheo, who had a pain in his forehead from drinking his milkshake too fast, just nodded. "Okay, Coach," Arturo said.

"When you two are rich, famous and pitching in the big leagues, I want you to remember your old Coach Mitchell."

Arturo and Cheo looked at each other, mouths open.

"I mean it," Coach said. "You two dopes keep your noses clean and work hard and you could go a long way." He was starting to choke up. He slapped his hand on the table and stood up. "And that goes for the rest of you jokers too. Got it? Now saddle up, we're out of here."

Arturo and Cheo went back to the field with City Island Pete to wait for his mother. Pete's mother looked like a fat lady who baked cookies except for her hair, which was blue and cut into a wide strip that ran down the middle of her head. She showed up in her minivan, waved to the other two while Pete climbed inside. "Yo, Cheo," Arturo said as they watched the van pull away. "You believe that, what Coach said about me and you?"

"I dunno," Cheo said. He had his old dirty baseball in his hand. The truth was, he was afraid to think about it. He was worried that he would jinx himself. "You?"

Arturo didn't answer right away. He was staring out across the ball field. "My moms works at the Post Office," he finally said. "You don't even get to see her in the mornings, she already be working. And then at night she works up to the Dollar Store. It ain't right."

"No," Cheo said. His mother worked pretty hard, too.

"I was thinking," Arturo said.

Cheo waited him out.

"You know you could make some serious money out on the corner."

"What do you mean?"

"Come on, man, you know what it is. White people from New Jersey, right, you know how they do. They come rolling up with they window down, they say 'Hey, bro,' like they know you or something. 'I need to find some weed, I want some blow,' or whatever they do. All's you gotta do is send them upstairs. Just, you know, 'yo, see that building, go on up to the fourth floor' or whatever. And then my moms could quit that Dollar Store, she hates it there and those people up in there, they hate her back."

"Carl Pavano signed for forty million bucks and your sister could pitch better than him," Cheo said.

"Cheo, you know those guys ain't like you and me."

"You was pretty good today," Cheo said.

"So was you. Who's these cats getting out of that van? They know you? Why they looking at us?"

Cheo dropped his milkshake. "We gotta run," he said. "Right now."

Arturo looked at him once and then the two of them ran.

Two guys, walking like they had urgent business, and they broke into a run as soon as Cheo and Arturo took off. One of them was on the doughy side, and he was the one who went after Cheo. The thinner guy, presumably faster, chased Arturo. The funny thing was, Arturo, though long and lean, was kind of a gawky kid and not very fleet of foot, but Cheo, who was much shorter, could really motor. He quickly outpaced them all, at least until he heard Arturo yell. Cheo, still carrying his old and dirty baseball, turned for a look, saw that Arturo's pursuer had caught him. Cheo took two more quick steps, then planted his right foot, turned and fired the ball, just like dealing a strike from short to first, he'd done it a thousand times. The pudgy guy coming after him cried out and pitched himself face-down in the grass but he wasn't the guy Cheo threw at. The guy holding Arturo didn't see the ball until almost too late, he ducked but not quite in time, the ball caught him high above his ear and caromed straight up. The guy sort of melted down to the ground and lay there wiggling his legs like a roach you'd just stepped on. Arturo jumped back to his feet and took off in a new direction, but unfortunately two more guys were waiting for him.

They each had a black hankie hanging halfway out of a back pocket.

The pudgy guy was back on his feet, huffing and puffing. He had no chance of catching Cheo, but the other two guys grabbed Arturo before he got very far. "You!" the guy said, pointing an unsteady finger at Cheo. "Get over here!"

Cheo thought about it. "Stay away from me," he said. "Don't you touch me, Chubbo, you try and I'll run your ass all over this field, you'll catch a heart attack and die, and then all your friends will die laughing at you." All he had to do was turn and run, but the other guys were already shoving Arturo into a van. Arturo, his teammate, who had thrown the other half of his shut-out.

"You see your buddy? You see him?" The guy was still sucking air. "You run now and I'll cut off his ears and send 'em to your mother. You hear me?"

Cheo stopped. Either way you lose, he told himself. But he couldn't run out on Arturo. "Don't touch me," he said as the guy got closer. "Stay away from me or I'll make you chase me for a hour, I swear to God."

The guy stopped and glared at him. "You rotten little bastard," he said, "you go get into the van and maybe we won't hurt your friend."

The guy Cheo beaned was back on his feet but he wasn't walking right. Cheo's pursuer looked over at his buddy, took a step in the man's direction, then stopped to glare at Cheo again. "G'wan!" he yelled. "G'wan and get in the truck!"

This is really stupid, Cheo thought, but he made a big circle around the pudgy guy, picked up his ball and headed for the van.

They had a huge pile of marijuana on a table in what used to be the dining room. It was an apartment in one of the projects and the place was trashed. Three guys were weighing the dope and packaging it into little baggies. The stench was overpowering, to Cheo it felt like some kind of mold had taken root in his sinuses and was growing up into his brain. The guy Cheo beaned was still down in the van, but the remaining three hustled Cheo and Arturo into one of the back rooms. It might have been a bedroom once but now there was nothing in it but a long folding table and some mismatched chairs. A heavily tattooed Black guy sat in one of the chairs. He looked like he smelled something bad. All three guys all began to try to tell the same story, and except for Cheo's pursuer, they thought it was very funny. After a while the tattooed man held up a hand and they all went silent at once.

"Ya cyan't even get one simple t'ing right," he said, irritated.

Jamaican, Cheo thought.

"I ax ya fa one damn child but ya got ta bring me two." He lumbered to his feet. "Raymond, you stay. You two, get on outa here. Ya make me sick. Go on, go on, get out!"

They shuffled out of the room, closing the door behind them and leaving Arturo and Cheo alone with Cheo's pursuer and his big Jamaican boss. The Jamaican walked over to Arturo, who stood stock still.

"'Im tell ya what 'im done?"

Arturo looked at the floor and shrugged.

The Jamaican stared at him in evident disgust. "Don' matter nohow," he said. "Too late for you. T'ank ya little friend ere, 'e the one that got ya inta this. G'wan an sit in na carna."

Arturo didn't move so the guy who had chased Cheo grabbed a handful of Arturo's shirt, dragged him to a corner and stuffed him into a chair.

The Jamaican looked at Cheo, pulled a chair away from the table. "Sit," he said. Cheo could feel his pulse racing as he walked over and sat down. The Jamaican took another chair and sat in it just inches away from Cheo. "Ya like baseball, do ya?"

"No," Cheo said, scowling at him. "I just like to wear uniforms."

"Very funny." The Jamaican reached out, tapped Cheo's right shoulder. "Ow about I have someone crack ya wit' da bat right dere on ya shoulda? T'ree, maybe four time. Bust ya shoulda into five hundred little bits. Ya never t'row a ball again."

"Wrong shoulder, Einstein," Cheo told him. "I'm a lefty."

The Jamaican stared at him in disbelief. "All right, ya little shit, 'ow 'bout I do 'em both? Hah? Den ya mama got ta feed ya wid' a spoon fa the rest a ya life. Wipe ye ass, too. 'Ow bout dat?"

Cheo kept his scowl. "Ga-head."

The Jamaican reached out and grabbed Cheo by the neck. "'Oo is 'e?"

"Pelios," Cheo told him, thrusting his chin forward. "The Greek. You mess with us and he'll kick your ass."

"I knew it!" The guy who'd chased Cheo sounded like he'd just found a twenty on the sidewalk. "I knew it!"

"Shut ye ass," the Jamaican told him. There was a sudden burst of noise from outside in the apartment, sounded like someone slamming car doors. The Jamaican let go of Cheo and leaped to his feet. "KNOCK OFF THE DAMN RACKET!" he bellowed at the door and the sounds died away. He sat back down, steaming. "Where is 'e?" he asked Cheo. "'Ow ya find 'im?"

"He finds me," Cheo said.

The Jamaican leaned in even closer. Cheo could smell his stank breath. "Where 'e live, huh? Where 'im sleep? Where 'im brush 'im teeth? Ya gonna tell me, boy. I promise ya. I promise."

Outside, the noises resumed and the Jamaican gritted his teeth. "Raymond," he said, without looking away from Cheo. "Get out dere and shut dem da hell up. Now. Right now."

The guy got up and left, closing the door carefully behind him.

"I know ya t'ink I be da bad guy 'ere. Let me tell ya somet'ing, kid. I am jus' like da man what own da liquor store, nuttin' more. Ya mama wan a little taste a somet'ing ta ease 'er pain, I sell to she. Jus' like da liquor store. Okay? I don' look ta 'urt no one. But Pelios! In Queens, where 'im live, everybody pray fa two t'ings." He ticked them off on his fat fingers. "One, God please don' let me die today, and two, God, please, in na eva-lovin' name a ya sweet son Jesus, please don' let me see dat sonuvabitch Pelios come t'rough my front door."

Cheo just stared at him.

The Jamaican lowered his voice to a whisper. "'Im kill da man 'oo raise 'im like 'im son, kill 'im fa da coupla pennies 'im got in the pocket. And I tell ya one t'ing more. Pelios, 'e sell 'imself to Lucifer. Even da Eye-talians is afraid of 'e. Mafia don' do no business down in Queens, right down ta dis very day. Ya wanna know why?" He nodded once, and his voice got even softer. "Pelios. Da Greek. Da money ya t'ink ya gonna make, it ain' wort' ya life, na ya mudda and ya fadda, ya wife an' ya little babies, ya sista and she t'ree cyat neither. Because Pelios, you cross 'im, 'e kill 'em all. So ya gatta tell me, son, where 'im lay 'im head, because we cyan' 'ave 'im runnin' loose."

Cheo thought about it. "Well, if he's so tough, how you gonna get him?"

The Jamaican shook his head. "No me-o, sonny boy, no me-o. But I 'ear of some bad people 'oo wan' very much ta send Pelios back down ta hell where 'im come from."

Cheo sat still and tried to figure what to do, but before he could make up his mind the door opened and Pelios limped into the room. He was dressed much nicer than the last time Cheo had seen him, he had a silver-tipped cane in one hand and a pistol in the other. He held the pistol upside down, by the barrel. He gestured at the Jamaican with the pistol. "Borrowed this from one your compadres out in the other room," he rasped. "He won't need it for a while."

The Jamaican seemed frozen.

"Nice game you pitched today, Lefty. Same for your buddy over there. I was impressed. Now get on out of that chair, go sit with your friend. I heard this gentleman was looking for me. He and I need to have a conversation about that."

The old man was about five foot nothing and seemed almost as broad as he was tall. He was not a fat guy, but blocky, like a gorilla. And he was a terrible driver. "My name is Gaitanis," he growled at Pelios. "That's what you call me. Gaitanis. Can you remember that?"

"Yes, sir."

Gaitanis stuck his unlit cigar stub back between his teeth. Pelios would rarely see him without it, that and his ever-present reading glasses perched high on his forehead. The light on Astoria Boulevard changed to green and the cars behind Gaitanis began honking but he paid them no mind. "You see that gas station over there?" he said, removing his cigar and pointing with it.

"Yes, sir."

"Mine," Gaitanis said. "You see that Dunkin' Donuts?"

"Yes, sir."

"Mine. Car wash, two blocks up. Diner, over on Northern Boulevard. Ice house down under the Tri-borough, and the truck garage right next to it. All mine. You see the connection?"

"They're all in Astoria?"

Gaitanis glared at him. "Cash business," he said, slowly, like Pelios was an idiot. "Cash. When a man hands you a check, all he's giving you is a promise. You hear me? This is the most important thing you'll ever learn. When a man hands you cash, you take it and you put it in your pocket. That's why I don't have no clothing stores, no trucking company, none of that. I don't like no checks, and I don't like no credit cards. I like cash money."

"Yes, sir."

Drivers were pulling out around Gaitanis' Mercedes, honking their horns and yelling. When the light turned yellow he finally woke up, tromped the gas and the heavy car lurched forward. "Nobody knows everything I got. Nobody. Not my sons, not my wife, not my girlfriends. Nobody." He pointed his cigar at his temple. "I know. Nobody else."

"Um, watch out, Mr. Gaitanis..."

Gaitanis stomped the brake just in time to avoid rear-ending the yellow cab that was waiting at the next light. "I seen him," he snapped. "Listen to me. I got a lotta people working for me. They never know when I'm gonna show up. Before they open up for the day, maybe. Three in the morning, sometimes. And they're all afraid." He jabbed his cigar in Pelios' direction. "They gonna try to give me the business? Well I give it to them first! And hard! That's why they're afraid."

Pelios wondered if he ought to be scared, too. "Yes, sir."

The light turned green and again Gaitanis ignored it. "If you are a smart kid," he growled, "I'll make you a rich man. I'll teach you everything. If you're stupid I'll put you right back on the corner. You hear me?"

"Yes, sir."

"You a smart kid?"

"Yes, sir." Pelios saw the doubt in Gaitanis' eyes. "You'll see," he told him.

Gaitanis seemed to like Pelios' confidence. "Okay," he said. "Listen to me. I have a tenant, he moved out early. Left me a check." He screwed his face up in *distaste. "The lady at the bank says 'Hey, we don't know this guy. No money in the account. Sorry.'"*

"Do you know where he went?" Pelios asked.

"No," the old man said. "But I know he works at the big sanitation garage down under the Long Island Expressway in Maspeth. Night shift. Leaves his car parked on the street outside all night long. I want it."

"You want me to steal his car?"

"Can you do it?"

"Yes, sir, but I don't have the tools."

"There's a parts guy right around the corner, we'll go there right now and get what you need."

"Okay."

Twenty minutes later Pelios had a nice shiny new slim-jim, a screwdriver and a slap-hammer. Whatever doubts he'd had about working for Gaitanis were silenced by the growling of his empty stomach.

Hunger usually makes a pretty convincing argument.

It was a mistake anyone could have made.

It's not smart to give in to fear, Cheo knew that so thoroughly that he no longer needed to put it into words, not even in his thoughts. If you think someone is following you on the street, you do not speed up, you slow down, as if to say, 'Yeah? You want a piece of this?' Natural caution is fine as long as nobody catches you using it. The Bronx is one of those places where giving in to fear can cost you everything.

Defiance was the wisest course, at least in Cheo's admittedly limited experience.

Besides, defiance was all he had.

Cheo glanced over at Arturo, who was staring at Pelios and the Jamaican.

Arturo was afraid.

It's only because I know Arturo, Cheo told himself. Otherwise I wouldn't be able to tell... Pelios had the Jamaican stand and he patted him down. In the hierarchy of fear, Arturo was afraid of the guys who'd chased them in the park. Those guys were afraid of the Jamaican, because they took his crap and did what he told them to do. And the

Jamaican was afraid of Pelios. He was trying not to show it, he stood with his jaw clenched and an arrogant look on his face but his eyes danced whenever something moved and his hands were shaking.

Satisfied the Jamaican was unarmed, Pelios sat him back down in the chair. He shook a finger in the man's face. "Don't you move," he said, and he winked at Cheo as he exited the room. As soon as he was gone the Jamaican looked around wildly but then he swallowed, subsided in his chair and stayed put.

Fear.

Can Pelios really be that bad? Cheo wondered. It would be a good thing to know. If Cheo crossed him would he really kill Cheo's mom's sister and her three cats?

Pelios was back a few seconds later with some short lengths of electrical wire. They all had plugs on one end, looked like he'd yanked them out of lamps and maybe the television set. He went around behind the Jamaican and used them to tie him to the chair. When he was done he went back around in front and sat in the chair Cheo had recently vacated. He lifted his bad knee and rested it on his other leg.

"My friend," he said. "How did you hear about me? Not from the street kids I rousted the other day. They left before I could make proper introductions."

"No," the Jamaican said.

"Come on, man," Pelios said. "Why not just do this the easy way? You know we'll get there in the end anyhow. Why make it hard on yourself?"

The Jamaican glanced at Cheo and Arturo.

"There's nobody here," Pelios told him. "The kids are with me. Nothing you say has to go past these walls. But you got to make up your mind quick. I don't have all day."

The Jamaican sighed and the stiffness seemed to go out of him. All of a sudden he looked shorter and fatter. "I 'ear yesterday," he said, looking down. "I 'ear ya was in the earea. Ya description match what me kids tell me, so I come fa ya boy, dere. I figure 'e gonna tell me where ya was."

"Well that was quick," Pelios said. "Who did you hear it from?"

The Jamaican shrugged. "One a your people," he said. "White guy in a suit. Come round axin' after ya. 'Im leave 'im cyard."

"I see. Greek, you think? You have the card?"

The Jamaican nodded at his shirt pocket.

"You don't mind, I'm sure," Pelios said, and he retrieved the card. He squinted at it. "Lawyers," he said. "What would we do without 'em? So how much was he offering?"

"Ten t'ousan if I tell 'e where ya lay ya head, come dark."

"Ten grand? What's a lousy ten large to a businessman like yourself?"

The Jamaican looked incredulous. "Ten t'ousan is ten t'ousan."

"Yeah, I guess you're right," he said, and he stood up. "When your boys come to, they'll untie you."

Cheo could see the sweat run down the Jamaican's temple. "No! Don't leave me like this! They'll cut my t'roat, you know they will!"

"Nice crowd you run with."

"Come on, man, you know how it is! Ya cyan't miss a step, dey be on ya like a pack a wile dogs! Please, mistah, I been square wit' ya..."

"Uneasy lies the head that wears the crown, huh?"

"Come on, don' talk shit, man, untie me or kill me quick, don't leave me like this! You know what they gonna do..."

"Yeah, you're right. Okay, tell you what. I'm gonna untie you and you can ride with us down in the elevator. Then I'll send you back up. After that, you stay away from me. And you stay away from my friend Lefty. Hear?"

The Jamaican stared at him, his face on the edge of panic.

"Relax. I don't want your blood on my hands," Pelios rasped. "But just so you and I are clear on this. I got a soft spot for ball players. You understand? You mess with these kids again, you're gonna answer to me. Got it?"

The Jamaican stared at him. "Ya just as crazy as dey said ya was."

"Are we clear?"

The Jamaican nodded. "On my life," he said.

Pelios sent the Jamaican back up in the elevator. "Okay guys," he said, "let's move. I wanna be out of sight before that guy gets to a window." The three of them left the building and headed for the nearest side street.

Once they were safely around the corner, Pelios slowed back down. He looked around. "What the hell happened to your buddy?"

"Arturo? He took off," Cheo said. "When we turned, he went straight up the block."

"Oh. Scared, I guess."

"Well, he didn't want a beef with the Black Hand Crew." Cheo wondered, again, just how smart this White guy was. "Because, you know, once you front them, they go get a gun and they come looking for you. And if they think you got a gun they'll get four more guys with guns and they'll all come for you at once. And if they find you they don't care if they hit just you or if they shoot some old lady walking her dog, and the dog, too."

It's all the kid knows, Pelios thought. This is normal for him... "Born and raised here, ain't you, Lefty. You ever get out of the city?"

"You mean, like, upstate?"

"No. Listen, I don't think you need to worry about those guys coming after you again."

"Why not?"

"When you step on a snake, you step on the head, not on the tail." What kind of a chance for an ordinary life does this kid have, Pelios thought. "We gotta get you back to playing baseball."

"Can I ax you something?"

"Can you ask me something, you mean."

The kid missed it. "Why you messing with these guys? You don't care nothing about them. You don't even live here. You live in like Manhattan or whatever. Am I right?"

"Something like that. Okay, Lefty, I'll tell you what I'm up to. Do you know how to catch a rat?"

"Poison him," Cheo said. "You put out them little blue pellets that you buy at the grocery, the rat eats them and he dies."

"That's one way, but that way you only get the rats dumb enough to eat the pellets. So ever since they started making those pellets, most of the dumb rats are dead already. The ones we got left now are mostly the smart ones."

"Too smart for a trap?"

"You mean one of those spring-loaded things? Yeah, I'm thinking the rat I'm looking for is too smart for that."

"So how you gonna get him?"

"You got to know what the rat likes. What he loves, actually. What he stays awake at night thinking about."

"Cheese," Cheo said.

"Nah, that's mostly from cartoons. You wanna know what rats really really love? Peanut butter."

"Serious?"

"Absolutely. So you take a bucket, okay, big plastic bucket, and you fill it halfway up with water. You put a dab of peanut butter on the inside of the bucket, right above the water line. Being that he's a smart rat, he knows he can't reach the peanut butter, okay, and he knows that if he tries for it he'll fall in and drown."

"So he goes away?"

"Yeah, maybe," Pelios said. "But he comes back. He has to. You know why? He loves peanut butter. I mean, he looooves peanut butter. He figures, hey, smart rat like me, there's gotta be a way I can get to that... And sure enough, in the morning you're gonna find one drowned rat in your bucket."

"Yuck," Cheo said. "Rat soup. Okay. So the guy in the suit that came looking for you, the one that offered the Jamaican ten grand, he's the rat."

"No. He's probably just the rat's lawyer. But the rat is coming. He can smell what he wants, and he won't be able to leave it alone. Come on, we gotta get you home."

"Okay. Can I ax you one more question?"

"Absolutely. Ask it while we walk up to the corner and find a cab."

"Those guys working for that Jamaican dude. Would they really hurt him? If he was still tied to that chair when they woke up."

"Yeah."

"Why?"

"Same reason the rat comes back for the peanut butter even when he knows he'll probably fall in and drown. It's because when you're a bad guy, or a rat, all you can think about is what you want. And the only thing those guys care about is money."

CHAPTER 3

Cheo's mother did not like it when the Yankees played an afternoon game, especially on a Saturday, especially when her favorite channel was running a marathon of 'Which Enormous House Are These Hideous Rich People Going To Buy?' She loved to sit in her chair and marvel at shiny wooden floors, walk-in closets, recessed lighting and three car-garages. She would root for the people on the show to buy the houses she liked best, cheer them when they agreed with her and call them 'idiota' when they did not.

"But I need to *see* the pitcher," he told her. "I won't learn nothing by just listening to him..." He did not understand why she liked the stupid show anyhow, he could not bring himself to watch it for more than a few minutes. In fact it irritated him so much he would do almost anything to get away, even take the garbage down.

On this particular Saturday, she relented.

Cheo sat forward on the edge of the couch scowling, concentrating on the pitchers. He watched the way they held the ball, he watched the way they wound up, he took note of exactly when they threw a curve, their throwing motions, and the way the ball cut in or out or down before it reached the plate.

"Why are you sitting there hating on that guy?" his mother asked him, sounding amused. "Did he just throw a touchdown against your team?"

"I know you just messing with me." He turned to look at her. It was the bottom of the fourth inning and he had not noticed her sitting there watching him watch the game. He tried to mold his face into a more acceptable shape. "This guy is throwing a circle change," he told her. "I just wanna see how he throws it. Look at the way he holds the ball, his finger and his thumb makes a circle on the side of it. See right there?"

"So what," she said.

"So the guy with the bat thinks the ball is coming like a hundred miles an hour, but it's not. He swings as hard as he can but he can't hit it."

"Can you do that?" He heard the wonder in her voice, it sounded for once like she was starting to get it.

"No," he said. "My hand isn't big enough yet. But now he's going to throw a curve. I can throw a curve. You hold the ball like this." He held his battered baseball in his left hand, gripping it the way Pelios had shown him. He squinted again, trying to pick up the pitcher's grip as he released the ball, which was not easy, especially when the camera cut away to show some dumb guy with his dumb kid eating hot dogs, which, you know, who cared? It was the bottom of the sixth when he remembered his mother watching him, but when he turned she was gone.

She came back at the top of the eighth. "Are you gonna sit there watching sports all day long?"

"No," said Cheo, who would have liked nothing better. "This game is gonna be over soon." The Yanks were losing big to Tampa Bay but Cheo was only mildly disgusted. Burnett had a nice curve going, Derek Jeter had gotten a single and a double but the pen fell apart late. You learned right away in baseball that sometimes the other guys won no matter what you did. He could almost hear Coach shouting, though. 'Don't try to hit a home run every time! Just get a base hit and drive in a run! Choke up on that bat, goddammit...'

And then it was over and his mother bogarted the remote. "Which one will they choose?" Suzanne Wong said. "Will it be house number one, with five bedrooms and four baths but the long walk to the beach, house number two with only four bedrooms but right on the water, or house number three...”

“I’m gonna go downstairs and practice,” Cheo told his mother. She usually didn’t mind him doing that, he could stay in the alley next to the building and throw against the brick wall down at the end. The Korean guy who ran the dry-cleaner on the other side of the block was a different story, though, because the back of the alley formed the back wall of his shop. But maybe if Cheo stuck to the curve, maybe the guy wouldn’t hear it...

“All right,” she said. “Take down the garbage.”

“Okay,” he said, and he sprinted for his bedroom. He slid across the bedroom floor on his knees, fished his glove out from under the bed without even looking and headed outside. She had the phone in her hand when he went by, he knew she was going to ask the super to keep an eye on him and like, for real, it’s Saturday afternoon, the guy is freakin’ cremated...

He forgot the trash.

First you had to be a groundskeeper...

At a regular game that meant Coach formed the team into a line to walk the outfield and throw all the rocks and bottles over the far end of the fence. For throwing practice it meant sweeping the center of the alley, for two reasons. First, you wanted the ball to take a nice true bounce when it came back at you, and second, you didn’t want your baseball covered in rat poop. Sometimes it also meant asking Mr. Berria, the super, to help you push the Korean’s Dumpster back out of the way, and good luck with that. Today, though, the baseball gods were smiling, because the dumpster was back in the corner where it belonged.

Cheo had a strike zone drawn in chalk on the back wall. One problem was that the zone was lower than normal because there was no mound to throw from. Cheo figured it stood to reason, you were standing lower so you had to hit a lower target. Sounded good anyway, but he wasn’t sure he was right. And besides, just above his imaginary strike zone a couple of bricks stuck partway out of the wall and if you hit one the ball would take a crazy bounce and you had to go chase it. The other problem was that Cheo was not sure if he was throwing from the right distance or not. He had counted off the steps from home plate to the pitcher's rubber at the field and then tried to duplicate the same distance in the alley but he always felt like he was still too close. Maybe that was because on an actual field the catcher would be farther back, behind the batter's box, but he could not be sure. It wasn't the best arrangement, but Cheo wanted to play baseball.

Sometimes you just had to find a way to make it work.

The first few throws were not pitches at all, they were just exploratory tosses to help him warm up his arm, find his range, and see if the Korean guy from the dry cleaners was going to come out and chase him away. Once he was satisfied with those preliminaries, he began working on his curve. He tried to picture a right-handed batter standing back behind the wall inside the batter's box, maybe a tall kid like the one who'd hit one out on him two games ago. Okay, he's crowding the plate a little bit... That meant Cheo had to nip the top right corner of his strike zone, right on the chalk. If the ump was fair he should get a called strike even if the batter was bailing out on him. And if your aunt had balls... But if he got the call he'd come back with the fastball low and outside, that would be his strikeout pitch because the batter would still be thinking about the previous pitch, much closer to his chin... In a real game they'd all be looking at him, both benches, the umpire, and even some of the parents and older brothers. He leaned over, squinted at City Island Pete's ghost for the sign, stood back up, came set, kicked high and threw... Too high, the ball clipped one of the bricks that stuck out and he had to go get it. That's all right, he told himself. Call it a base hit. That put an invisible man on first with nobody out, not a good way to start a game, but Cheo wasn't worried. And anyhow, he had to get his curve ready, who knew when you were going to need it? The next curve was down where he wanted it, he could see the ball spinning on its way to the zone. Call that one a strike... You could play an imaginary game with three guys because it was fair, if you had a real batter and he got a hit, he got a hit, that way you knew for sure what bases your invisible baserunners were on. In Cheo's alley, though, everything was possible except a fair game because it was too easy to imagine that you were striking everybody out. Plus, Cheo didn't want to chance throwing the down and away fastball for real because you didn't want the game called on account of a pissed-off Korean.

He got as far as two on, two out because the curve was a lot harder to locate than the fastball. Besides, in a real game he wouldn't be throwing the curve that much, in a real game he would probably be out of the inning by now... Yeah, sure, he told himself. You got two on, two out, sucka, no fair cheating, if you don't strike this next guy out it's one-zip. He leaned over again, squinted in for the sign...

He heard voices, and he ran. Even if you weren't doing anything wrong, innocence was no excuse, not on his block. He made it down to the end of the alley and slid in low behind the Korean's reeking Dumpster. He bent down and peered underneath, counted four pairs of legs walking up the alley. Two of the legs were wearing high heels. "Are we really gonna pay this guy?" a man's voice said.

"Shut up, Gregory." It was a woman's voice.

"But what if.."

"I said, shut it," the woman said, emphatic.

And then someone pounded on the basement door, the one that led into the room where Mr. Berria, the building super, slept.

After they went inside, Cheo waited a couple of minutes to make sure it was safe to come out. He thought about going back upstairs, even considered going inside to watch HGTV with his mother, but ultimately he decided that it wouldn't be safe, mostly because of Pelios and the rats he was trying to catch. The Jamaican had already tried once to get to Pelios through Cheo, how could he be sure that it wasn't going to happen a second time? He ran back up the alley, entered his building through the front door and eased down the steps to the cellar. There were two washing machines and two driers down there, as well as a boiler room and the room where the super lived, and far back in the corner there was a room with a water heater in it, if you went in there you could hear Mr. Berria's television like you were sitting on his couch next to him. Cheo generally avoided it because the lights didn't work and the place hadn't been cleaned out the whole time he and his mother had lived in the building, which was like forever, and who knew what could be hiding in there? But he heard voices when he got to the doorway so he went in.

"How come you din' bring the money?" It was Berria's voice, complaining, the guy was even more loaded than usual, Cheo could tell from the way he talked. "I already tol' you everything. When you and me talk on the phone, Missy, you said..."

A woman's voice, low and soothing, answered him. "Don't worry, Mr. Berria, I'm going to take good care of you. Just go through it again so my brother and his friends can hear. Tell them exactly what you told me. Okay? Can you do that?"

"Sheesh. All right, all right. Pelios come here four nights ago. Slep' right on that couch."

"Straight out of the joint?" It was a male voice and it sounded harsher than the woman.

"I dunno, man, he din' say. We had a few beers, you know, talked about the ol' days. I ax him if he was looka for a job, he jus' laugh at me. Said he din' have no money problems."

"Son of a... I knew it!" a second man's voice said.

"Gregory, I told you to shut it." It was her again. "I'm not going to tell you again." The place went silent for a moment, the loudest thing Cheo could hear was the rasping of his own breath, to him it was louder than a train coming into a subway station. "I'm sorry, Mr. Berria. You were telling us about that first night with Pelios. Please continue."

"What else can I tell you? We drink some beers..."

"You did talk about money, though. Isn't that right?"

"Some. Pelios said he din' need nothing. Said he got everything he need. I said, you make plenty, back inna day. Yeah, he tells me. So how come the state don' take it all when they send you up, I ax him. He says, if they can't find it, they can't take it. Says the old man teach him good. Yeah, I say, that old man, he was one rich bassard. Own the car wash, the gas station, I thin' he own the diner, too. That was nothing, Pelios says. That shit was jus' for show."

Someone inhaled sharply.

"I'm sorry." Her voice was so low Cheo had to strain to hear it. "I didn't quite catch that last part. Could you please..."

"Jus' for show. That money was for the wife, and to pay some tax. Keep everybody happy. The real money come from the airpor'."

"What airport?"

"Both of 'em. LaGuardia and Kenney. Kenneny."

Kennedy, you bum, Cheo thought.

"The old man got a piece of everything that come in. Say you try to sneak a couple keys of weed into New York and you din' give him none, the baggage hannelers take it, okay, and maybe Pelios and the old man take you for a nice fishing trip to the bottom of Jamaica Bay." Berria cackled and immediately Cheo knew why he never liked the guy: the sound of his laugh spoke of all the rum Berria had drunk, all the cigars he'd smoked, all the evil he'd done.

"Are you saying... Do you know this for sure or is it just talk?"

Berria's wheezing cackle sounded again, longer this time. "Don' forget, me an' Pelios, we work together lilla bit, back inna day. He could always truss me. He come right to me, dinnee? When he got out. I gotta go diving in Jamaica Bay someday. Gotta be a hunnert bad guys down under there."

She cleared her throat. "Let's get back to the money," she said. "You say Pelios told you he had some salted away somewhere."

"Thass right."

"What about the old man's money? Do you think he knows where it is?"

"He knows," Berria said. "He knows. I tell you what. He don' have not even one drink for twelve year, so late that night we was both dronk off our ass. 'The eyes,' he says to me. 'The eyes tell you where to look.' And then he pass out sleeping."

"The eyes?" a male voice said. "What the hell is that supposed to mean?"

Two voices answered him in unison. "Shut up, Gregory!" It was the woman and one of the other men.

"You know somethin,' ten thou don' seem like a whole lotta dough," Berria said. "You know what I'm sayin.' If you find the old man's money buried down there in Queens somewhere, right, iss because I tol' you where to find Pelios. It was me that call you, remember..."

"We'll take good care of you, Mr. Berria. Just a few more things. Have you seen Pelios again since that first night?"

"No, uh-uh," Berria said. "But he's around."

"How do you know?"

"He had a beef with one a the gangs up here."

"What kind of a beef?"

"I dunno, it din' make no sense to me. 'The Black Hand,' thass what they call theirself. I hear they grab two kids. Lill Leaguers."

"The Black Hand? I never heard of them. Why would Pelios care about a coupla kids?"

"Beas'a shit outa me. He knew one of 'em, maybe. I hear he walk right in to where the Black Hand was and lay 'em all out cold."

"He killed them all? I didn't hear anything, something like that would make the news, surely..."

"No." Berria sounded surprised. "Din' kill nobody. Guy tol' me Pelios put 'em all down with a sap."

"That don't sound reasonable," a man's voice said. It sounded like Gregory again, but this time nobody told him to shut up. "That don't sound like the Pelios we all know and love."

"They couldn't have known what they were up against," the woman's voice said. "Mr. Berria, do you know who the kids were?"

Cheo stopped breathing.

"Nah. Jus' couple street rats."

Cheo tried to swallow but his mouth was dry.

"Well, thank you, Mr. Berria. I think we're almost done with you," the woman's voice said.

"Wait, hole up there sugarcakes, you said you was gonna..." And then there came a horrible retching noise that seemed to go on and on, and some muffled thumps, like someone kicking the floor with sneakered feet. And then a while later, a bigger thump, like someone falling to the floor.

"Yeah, I can see Pelios sweating over some neighborhood kid," one of the men said. Someone laughed.

Cheo heard them heading for the door. "If he was worrying about a kid from the neighborhood," the woman's voice said, "I would bet my house he had a damned good reason. He's using the kid for something."

Cheo heard the super's door open and then there she was, framed in the faint light coming through the doorway into the water heater room. Tall, long dark hair, pale skin, she was beautiful. Cheo froze, praying she wouldn't see him back in his dark corner.

"Well, that was fun, I been wanting to strangle someone ever since my divorce." It was the one they called Gregory, Cheo couldn't see him but he'd come to recognize the voice. "Now all we gotta do…"

She reached into a purse, pulled out a small thin silver knife, then all at once she whirled and struck. There was another horrible retching noise as she leapt back. "Hold him!" she cried. "Hold him still! Until he bleeds out." Someone just out of Cheo's view let out a strangled cry, and then the guy started crying for real, crying lost and heartbroken like a baby does when he's all alone, and he seemed to go on forever, Cheo was finding it hard not to cry himself, and then finally the crying dissolved into a sort of wet cough that got steadily weaker, and then briefly, what sounded like someone trying to breathe underwater. The woman stood there half out of Cheo's view, staring as Gregory, unseen, died.

"Blood spatter," a man's voice said. "Get any on ya?"

"Probably," she said. "God, I'd hate to have to throw these shoes out. You have any idea how long it took me to find these in my size?"

"You were a little harsh, don't you think?"

"Gregory was going to sell us out to Pelios the first chance he got."

"How do you know that? And what could he say to Pelios?"

"I just know. We couldn't take the chance. Have you forgotten what Pelios is capable of? Or do you think perhaps prison has made him soft? Besides, I told Gregory three times to shut up," she said. "He didn't listen."

"Yeah. You know, I never really liked him much anyway. What's next?"

She turned and walked out of Cheo's view, presumably heading for the basement stairs. Two men walked past Cheo's doorway. Cheo strained to hear what her answer was going to be. He couldn't quite be sure, but it sounded like 'Find that kid.'

· · ·

Cheo stayed silent in the water heater room for a long time. The two men right outside the door were quieter still. Cheo's thought back to the other times that Death had paid an unannounced visit to Valentine Street, as casual and unexpected as his mother's sister who would drive over from Jersey, complain about no manners, no parking spots and no good delis, and then depart. When Cheo was nine a woman who lived on the second floor had overdosed in her apartment, booze and oxy's ending a life so dark and lonely that, for a while, no one even noticed her missing. Cheo could no longer remember what she'd looked like, only the smell in the hallway outside her door. Not long after that someone had robbed a gypsy cab driver and left him dead in his car right out in front of the building. And just recently two guys a year older than Cheo had gone swimming in The Bronx River. There was a water falls near the Botanical Garden, you had to climb over a fence to swim there, and the falls had trapped one of them underwater and drowned him. The second one had died trying to save his friend. And then there had been the kid from the T-Mac Nine, just the other day…

But this was the first time Death had passed so close Cheo had been able to smell her breath.

He finally moved because something else did first, some other basement occupant, presumably a mouse or a water bug. He stepped carefully, breathless, as though any sudden move would shatter him.

Gregory lay on his side in a pool of blood outside the door to Berria's room. In life Cheo had only seen his feet. Cheo took a breath, went through the door and backed away toward the basement stairs. Berria's door was open wide and Berria was inside his room sitting on the floor with his back up against his ratty couch, his face frozen in wide-mouthed horror.

Upstairs, Cheo's mother knew the instant she saw him that something was up.

"What happened?" she said. "Tell me."

CHAPTER 4

He left out a few details. After all, his future as a Cardinal hung in the balance... He didn't say anything about Pelios, or the Jamaican and the Black Hand. Maybe it wasn't exactly lying but still, he didn't feel great about it. And she did question him for a long time.

He waited until she seemed like she was done. "Are we gonna call the police?" he asked her.

"Now you listen to me," she said, and she shook a finger at him. "What those people do to each other is none of our business. And anyway this is what happens when you drop out of school and go sell drugs on the corner. Those kids might all have I-Pods and cell phones and two hundred dollar basketball shoes, but they don't have no future! They're never going to be anything! Every last one of them is going to wind up dead or in jail or..."

It was a lecture Cheo had heard many times. He did not question the truth of it, but what he took from it this time was the comforting thought that she wanted him to keep his trap shut, that he didn't need to worry about calling the police because any minute now one of the other ladies from the building would go down there to do her laundry and it would be safe for her to call because she didn't know anything and she wouldn't get into any trouble, probably.

Cheo couldn't sleep.

He sat on his bed and stared out into The Bronx night. The Yankees were finishing up their west coast trip but he made no move to turn on his radio, instead he sat wishing he could time-travel back a few days, back to when his biggest problem was the umpire who wanted all the little kids to get a hit.

At least now he knew why Pelios had not been afraid of the street kids...

He remembered the feel of the hard skin on Pelios' hands when he'd showed Cheo how to throw the curve. If somebody was really a bad person, would he bother to teach you a thing as good as that? Would a bad guy even care about some stray kid about to catch a beating on his way home from a ball game? One thing Cheo did know for sure, the people who'd killed Berria and Gregory earlier that evening were bad news, and even they were afraid of Pelios. He remembered what the woman had said: 'Have you forgotten what he's capable of?' Cheo had her figured for the smart one, and if that was true, he ought to be worried. She had been sure that Pelios was using Cheo for something.

Great. Just great.

He reached down to the floor next to his bed and fished his baseball out of his glove. He held the ball the way Pelios had shown him. He was getting it, he knew he was, pretty soon he'd have enough control over the curve to use it in a real game, and that would make him a pitcher, a real one, and not just a guy who threw the ball to the catcher as hard as he could.

Someone knocked on the door, Cheo sat with his heart in his throat and listened hard while his mother answered it. There was a guy in a police uniform in the hallway. "We're just canvassing the building, maam," the cop said. "Can you tell us anything about Mr. Berria, your superintendent? Did you hear or see anything unusual earlier this evening?"

"What has he done now?" his mom said, even though she knew the guy was already dead. Cheo felt both relieved and disappointed that she was so good at lying. The cop didn't give her much and she gave him back even less, but she made the appropriate noises at the right times. "Oh, that's awful," she told the guy, and after some more talking he went away.

Cheo heard noises out in the alley and he got up off his bed to go look. Some guys were wheeling a gurney out of the building. There was a long shape on the gurney, probably one of the dead guys, zipped up in a bag. Neither Berria nor Gregory could have known that their number was up, Berria had been all worried about getting the money they'd promised him and Gregory was thinking about more or less the same thing, what were they going to do to get the money they thought Pelios had. In a way, the Jamaican had been right, because it wasn't worth the money... Right then the realization struck Cheo that Berria had been killed in the act of selling out his old friend Pelios for ten thousand dollars, money he did not get to see, let alone spend. Cheo figured, if there really was a hell, that ought to get you a ticket there for sure.

Maybe this whole thing is over, Cheo thought. Part of him really wanted to believe that it was but most of him was pretty sure it wasn't. Pelios had gotten two rats already, they had seen the water but they went for the peanut butter anyhow, just like he'd said they would, and they'd fallen in and drowned.

He was still sitting there on his bed early the next morning when someone knocked on the door. "Cheo, will you get that?" his mother called.

He knew it wasn't over as soon as he opened the door. Two guys stood out in the hallway and looked at him. One was an older White guy in a gray suit and a tie, the other guy was younger, he had olive skin, long black hair in a ponytail and tattoos on the backs of his hands. His left thumbnail was longer than any of his fingernails. He smiled when he saw Cheo.

"You must be Lefty," he said.

· · ·

Cheo's mother didn't flip out the way he thought she would, she didn't yell and scream. Instead she pulled out her big gun: she came into the room and stared at him hard, looking hurt, betrayed and disappointed.

He felt like a cockroach.

"What have you been hiding from me?" she said.

"Mrs. Hernandez." It was the older cop, the guy in the suit. "Your son hasn't done anything wrong. And we didn't come here to cause trouble for you or for him. Would you mind if we stepped inside and had a talk?" She walked over and held the door open for them, but she kept hitting Cheo with The Look, the one that made him feel like the biggest dirtbag in the world. She motioned the two policemen to sit on the couch while she fetched two chairs from the kitchen. She sat in one, pointed at the other. "Sit down," she said. "Lefty."

I'm dead, Cheo thought. I should just go up to the roof and jump off. Get it over with.

"I'm Vernon Glass," the cop in the suit said. "This is my partner, Cesar Alcantare. We're with the Greater Queens Organized Crime Task Force."

Cheo's mom looked at Glass, then at Alcantare, then Cheo. "What's he done," she said.

Glass sighed and looked away. Alcantare leaned forward. "Mrs. Hernandez," he said, "my partner disagrees with me on this, but since I'm working undercover on this case, sometimes I get my way, and I feel strongly that it's only fair that we level with you about what Lefty is involved in."

She stared at Cheo.

"It's not his fault, Mrs. Hernandez, the only thing he did was stand up to some gangbangers. You should be proud of him. He's got a pair."

"Cesar..." Glass growled.

"Pardon me. I should have said, he's got guts."

"I know what you meant," Cheo's mom said.

"I'm sorry. Please excuse my language. Anyway, let me tell you a story. Up until about thirteen years ago, Astoria, in Queens, was a very safe neighborhood. You could walk the streets without worrying you'd get mugged."

"Greek neighborhood," Cheo's mom said.

"That's right. Large Greek population, but that's not the reason why the crime rate was so low. The real reason was a man named Gaitanis."

"A godfather?" she asked.

"Not exactly. To be honest, we're still not entirely clear on all of Gaitanis' criminal activities. His name never really showed up on police radar until the early nineties. In ninety-three his Mercedes was reported stolen by a woman who apparently had a relationship with him. Well, the car was spotted and a traffic stop was initiated but Gaitanis was riding in the car, which was being driven by an eighteen year old male named Lazur Pelios. There was an unlicensed .38 special under the driver's seat, which Pelios claimed was his. We didn't believe him, we suspected that he was covering for Gaitanis but we couldn't shake his story. He wound up doing just over a year and a half for the gun."

"What does this have to do with my son?"

"I'm getting to that. To answer your original question, though, Gaitanis was not really a 'godfather' type figure. We don't think he engaged in criminal activities directly, other than extorting monies from anyone who operated in his neighborhood. For example, if you wanted to sell dope in Astoria, either you paid Gaitanis or you disappeared."

"I know what extortion means."

"No disrespect, Mrs. Hernandez, I just wanted to be clear. Now, what has caused our present difficulties, Gaitanis was a funny guy. He didn't trust banks. I don't mean just the savings and loan down on the corner, I mean financial institutions of any kind. We're pretty sure that he was an immensely wealthy man, but we could never figure out what he did with the money. He didn't have anything in the market at all."

"I don't keep my money in the stock market either," Cheo's mom said.

"I know exactly what you mean. My ex-wife handles most of mine, the rest of it I waste on food and shelter. Listen, I know this is a long story so I'll cut to the chase. Gaitanis was shot and killed in '98 in an apartment house he owned in Long Island. This was a couple of years after Pelios did his stretch for the gun. He was apprehended leaving the scene with the murder weapon in his jacket pocket."

"This guy Pelios? First he goes to jail for his boss, and then he shoots him?"

"Exactly. But he wouldn't crack, he wouldn't say a word to us. The DA thought he had a good case and he decided to prosecute. Pelios wouldn't even enter a plea, the judge had to do it for him. He was found guilty and served over twelve years for manslaughter. He got out a week ago."

"Okay. So?"

"So now the topic of Gaitanis' money has become, in certain circles, one of those urban myths. You know, like alligators in the sewer. Millions of dollars worth of gold, or diamonds, or coke, or you name it, buried in a hole somewhere in Queens. After Gaitanis was killed, his house in Astoria was broken into and ransacked so many times that his widow finally sold out and moved back to Greece. And the same sort of thing happened at any other location that seemed likely, like the building where he died, a gas station that he owned, and so on and so forth."

"So why aren't you guys down in Queens looking for it? Why are you up here in The Bronx?"

"Because when Pelios was released from prison, he didn't go to Queens. He came to The Bronx."

"Oh. And now everybody thinks he hid the money up here."

"Precisely. Or that Gaitanis did, and that Pelios knows where it is. And the fact is, Mrs. Hernandez, we're sort of, ah, considering that possibility ourselves. And finally, the part that specifically concerns you, Pelios seems to have taken an interest in your son."

"In Cheo?" She came alive at that, horror written plain on her face. "Why? He's only..." She looked at Cheo. "I mean..."

"Mrs. Hernandez." It was Glass. "Criminal enterprises are remarkably similar to legitimate businesses. They need workers, so they look for kids who are tough, smart and know how to keep their mouths shut. According to the safety officers at PS117, your son Lefty fits that profile admirably. They also told us that one of the local gangs has targeted him for recruitment but he's been holding out."

She whirled on him. "You didn't tell me? These people are after you? Why didn't you..." But she knew the answer to that, he could see it on her face. If he'd said a word, she'd have locked him in his room forever.

No more baseball.

As it was, things were not looking too swinging for the rest of his season. "They didn't ax me to go with them. They was just frontin' me."

"Mrs. Hernandez, if I may." It was Glass again. "It seems a few days ago Lefty was being harassed by some of the gang members and Pelios, who was passing by, decided to do some harassment of his own." He looked at Cheo. "Am I right?"

Cheo didn't want to answer.

"It's all right," the cop told him. "You're not in any trouble here."

"Easy for you to say," Cheo said.

Alcantare laughed until he noticed Glass staring at him.

"Answer the man," Cheo's mother said through gritted teeth.

Cheo shrugged. "They was doing what they do. Pelios made them stop."

"Why can't you just find this Pelios character and arrest him?" Cheo's mother said.

"We can't do that," Glass said. "He served his time and he's a free man. We can put a tail on him, sure, but until he gives us a reason to arrest him..."

"What's it going to take?" she said. "Are you telling me we have to wait until he murders someone else? How does that make any sense?"

"Well hopefully it won't come to that," Alcantare said. "In the short term, our intention is to monitor him as closely as we can. After all, he's given us no reason to think that he isn't going to return to his former behaviors, and if that's the case, we'll have him back inside sooner rather than later."

"Oh, terrific," she said. "That makes me feel loads better. Where does that leave my son? What about Cheo? What about these people who've been harassing him?"

"I doubt they'll be a problem any more," Glass told her. "With your permission, we'd like to keep an eye on Lefty. Quietly, of course. He can go about his normal activities, but we'll try to have someone watching whenever we can. He probably won't even notice us, and neither will anyone else. This would serve two purposes. First of all, and most importantly, it will help us do everything we can to ensure his safety, and second, we think it may lead us to Pelios. We want to know more about what he's doing and who he's talking to."

"Do you think it was Pelios who killed those two downstairs?" she said.

The two cops looked at each other. "How'd you know there was two of them?"

"Get off it," she snapped. "Did you really think you could keep something like that hushed up?"

"Jungle telegraph," Glass said to Alcantare. Cheo saw the muscles in his mother's jaw clench up. She felt insulted whenever somebody dissed her neighborhood.

Alcantare saw it, too. "Actually we didn't want to publicize the fact that there were two deaths," he said hastily. "And no, we don't know whether Pelios did it or if it was someone else, but believe me we're working on it. If you're asking my opinion, I think it's too much of a coincidence that Pelios gets released, turns up in this neighborhood and then a couple of days later two ex-cons die in a basement."

Cheo's mother looked at him and he watched her closely. He knew that it hadn't been Pelios who killed the two in the basement the night before but if she wanted him to tell Glass and Alcantare what he'd seen, she would tell him so, otherwise he was keeping his mouth shut. In a place like The Bronx, informing on anyone, to anyone, was almost as smart as pulling on a stray dog's tail. Nobody would feel sorry for you when you got bitten.

She looked away, out the window. "Sometimes I hate this city," she said.

"Mrs. Hernandez," Alcantare said, "I promise you that I will do everything in my power to ensure that nothing happens to Lefty."

"Thank you," she said. Cheo wasn't sure she was buying in, but then she surprised him. "He's a good boy," she told Alcantare. "He'll do the right thing. But watch over him. You watch him good."

"You have my word."

Glass looked at Cheo. "Do you have any questions you'd like to ask us?"

"Um, yeah." Cheo glanced at his mother.

"Go on," she said.

He sucked in a big breath, held it, let it out. "You guys, um, you talked to that Jamaican dude. That guy from the Black Hand."

Cheo's mother wrung her hands but said nothing. The two cops glanced at each other. "Yes," Alcantare said. "We did. How did you know that?"

"That's how you knew to call me Lefty."

"Yeah. The Jamaican heard Pelios calling you that. Anything else?"

"Yeah. If you're a real policeman, how come you got a coke thumbnail?"

Alcantare looked at his hand. "Makes me look like a user, doesn't it?"

"Yeah," Cheo said. "And the tattoo, the cross near your thumb."

"Got that in Attica," Alcantare said.

"You went to jail? And they still let you be a policeman?"

"I was a cop before I went to Attica," Alcantare said. "I was still a cop while I was inside. And I was a cop when they let me out. When you work undercover, Lefty, it means the bad guys you're after have to really really believe that you're one of them. That's part of my job. We don't have anybody inside the Black Hand because they're too small, but the NYPD has officers inside the Bloods, we've got officers who are members of the Aryan Brotherhood, the Latin Kings, the Russian mob, what's left of the Mafia... We've got people working undercover all over the world. I heard we even have two guys inside Al Qaida. You wanna know why? It's because New York is our city. If someone is planning on doing us dirty, we wanna know about it first. We're not going to sit at home hoping that the FBI or someone else is going to protect us. That's not the way it works, not in this city. We take care of our own business, we don't rely on anyone else to do our job for us. I have never stopped being a cop, not ever. And when I finish my assignment, I'll cut off this thumbnail, and I'll get these tattoos removed, I'll cut my hair and I'll even dress up in a suit like Detective Glass, over there, except I'll look good in mine."

Cheo figured he was supposed to laugh at that, but he didn't. "What do you want me to do?" he said.

The two cops both exhaled at the same time. "You just keep to your normal routine," Alcantare told him. He reached into a pocket and pulled out a tiny cell phone, handed it over. "But carry this with you. Don't let anybody see it. When and if Pelios contacts you, you call me as soon as you can do it without being seen. Here, let me show you how this thing works...."

After they left, Cheo's mother sat on the couch next to him and combed his hair with her fingers. She didn't cry and she didn't say anything. Cheo's mind raced, he had a thousand questions but something told him to stay quiet so he kept them bottled up. The faint sounds of a radio filtered in through an open window. Cheo could hear voices from downstairs speaking in a language that he did not recognize. Finally he heard a smack, the all-too-human sound of an open hand striking flesh, followed quickly by what sounded like a child, crying. That seemed to rouse Cheo's mom out of the spell she'd been under. She patted Cheo on the head and then withdrew her hand. "Your aunt wants us to move to Jersey," she said.

"Jersey?" Cheo couldn't believe it. "Why would we wanna go to Jersey?" he said, horrified. He looked up to see that she was wearing a sad smile.

"Safer neighborhoods. Better schools. She thinks we'd be better off there. Maybe we'd have a future."

"But is there... Do they have anybody like me and you in Jersey? They'll probably hate us there."

"No, baby, they don't have anybody like you, anywhere. But there are plenty of Puerto Ricans in Jersey, if that's what you're worried about. The kids wouldn't all hate you. We'd have to stay in your aunt's basement until we could get on our feet. I'd have to find a new job, and get my driver's license, and..."

As always, Cheo was suspicious of anything new. "I don't wanna go to Jersey."

She sighed. "I don't think I do, either, baby, but this neighborhood is not what it used to be. You used to be able to walk down the street at night."

Somehow Cheo knew that what Alcantare had told him was right, you had to be careful not to go trusting that other people were going to take care of you. You had to take care of your own business.

And he'd been thinking... "I'm going to quit Little League."

"Oh, no, baby..." She drew him close to her. "No, don't you dare. You have to live, honey, you can't hide up in here with me." She sniffed. "I'm going to find out how much it costs for driving lessons, and maybe we'll go and look at your aunt's basement. And maybe I'll go to church Sunday and ask God to watch over you." She saw the look of distress on his face and she sighed. "Don't worry, you don't have to come."

"You don't want me to quit baseball?"

She shook her head. "The police are going to be watching you. And so will I, whenever I'm not working I'll walk you over to practice and home again. God is going to be watching you, too."

Somehow Cheo didn't relish being the center of all that attention, but at least it sounded like he might get to pitch again.

CHAPTER 5

Real alley cats don't strut.

Real alley cats stay out of the middle of the sidewalk, they avoid open spaces, and they watch everybody and everything. Real alley cats work the margins. That's how they stay alive.

The streets of The Bronx seemed colder than usual to Cheo that morning. He felt eyes watching him with every step he took. He eyeballed every person out walking or waiting for the bus, he tried to watch the people in all the passing cars but he couldn't tell if anyone was looking at him for real or not. He looked for the two cops, Glass and Alcantare, but he didn't see them anywhere. He did see one limping figure cross the avenue ahead of him but it was only an old homeless guy pushing a shopping wagon half filled with empty beer cans.

No Pelios.

No cops either, not that he could see.

Then it hit him.

All these stinking rats Pelios is after, he thought, they all think I have the peanut butter...

This is just great.

He ducked into the next bodega he came to, nobody else inside except for the guy behind the counter, who eyed him suspiciously. "What you wan'?" the guy said.

Cheo stared out through the glass door. "Some guy in a van," he lied. "He was trying to get me to go with him." He was wasting his time, he realized, because the glass of the door was too dirty and scratched to see through with any clarity.

"Ya got any money?" the counterman demanded. "Ya don' got no money, ya just come ta steal from me. If ya don' got no money, gwan, get outa here. Buy something or get out!"

Cheo turned and glared at the guy, his hand on the door. "Thanks pal," he told the guy. "If that creep gets me, it's on your head, you know that?"

"Get out!" the man shrieked, and he ran around the end of his counter. "Goddam rotten thieving kids!"

Cheo hit the door and burst back out onto the sidewalk.

For the first time in his life he was sorry he was wearing his baseball uniform because it made him stand out so clearly. Probably could spot him a mile away... The hell with it, he thought. Let them catch me. He gritted his teeth, stuck out his jaw, and marched, all the way to the bus stop.

His mood did not improve much when he got to the ball field. He was early and the gate was still locked, but some older kids had hopped the fence and were playing a lame imitation of a softball game, one batter, two kids shagging balls in the outfield, one kid pitching. Cheo climbed up and sat on a mailbox to watched the pitcher, who threw like he had no clue. Every time he missed the general vicinity of the strike zone the batter had to go chase down the ball and throw it back, and he was getting sick of it. "Come on, dumbass," the batter yelled. "Put it where I can reach it or I'll ask El Tiante over there on the mailbox to come and do it for you."

The pitcher looked around for El Tiante, saw only Cheo. "What are you looking at?" he yelled. He had to know that Cheo's presence meant that the Little League games would be starting soon and his time on the field was limited. "Get lost, before I come smack you!"

Cheo just stared at him.

"Go on, beat it! Don't make me climb over that fence!"

"Oh, yeah?" Cheo snarled back, suddenly furious. "Who you kidding? You didn't climb over to get in, you hadda walk all the way down to the corner outfield where the fence has a hole, didn't you? Come on, let's see your stupid ass climb the fence! Come on, I'm waiting!"

The pitcher took two steps in Cheo's direction but you could see on his face that he knew it was hopeless. Cheo didn't move. The batter and the two kids in the outfield were all laughing at him now. He turned and yelled at the two in the outfield. "Shut up! Shut up, you guys!" They, being at a safe distance, began to taunt him. He turned from them to the batter. "Shut up!"

The batter doubled over, laughing. "Go ahead, climb over," he said. "I wanna see it too! Climb over!" The pitcher pegged the softball at him and the batter danced back out of the way, then came after the pitcher, hefting his bat. The pitcher turned to run but he wasn't built for it, the batter caught up to him near first base and cracked him across the rear end with the bat.

"AAAAAAAAAGH!"

The pitcher went down, bellowing. The batter stopped to watch. The pitcher kicked at him from his prone position down in the infield dirt, but the batter jumped back and swung his bat again, threatening. The pitcher kicked again but missed wildly. After a few minutes the batter tired of the game, and with a backward glance at Cheo he headed off through the outfield where he and the two other kids went through the hole in the fence and drifted away.

The pitcher lay in the dirt by first base, crying.

Tough game, softball.

"Hey, kid!" With her blue mohawk, City Island Pete's mom did not exactly look like an angel of mercy and she didn't sound like one either. "What the hell is wrong with you?" She unlocked the chain that held the gate shut and kicked it open. "Get outa here! We got little kids coming to play a game, so whatever you're doing, go do it somewhere else."

City Island Pete shook his head and looked up at the sky in silent supplication. The softball pitcher lumbered to his feet, his eyes crusted with dirt, and he looked around for someone to blame. "He hit me!" he bawled, and he pointed at Cheo. "He said, he said I couldn't play here, and he hit me!"

Pete's mom looked over at Cheo. "Him? You talking 'bout Cheo? You kidding me or what? Big tub a shit like you, you let one scrawny little Puerto Rican hit you so hard you lay there on the ground blubbering like a little girl? That what you're saying? Go on, get outa here, we got a game."

"He had a baseball bat!" the kid shouted, outraged. "He, he had a bat, and he hit me with it!"

She looked over at Cheo again. "I don't see no bat."

"He threw it away! He tossed it so he wouldn't get in trouble! I'm gonna go find a cop!" He took a step in her direction but she still had the chain in her hand and she gave it a little shake.

"Cheo don't got no bat. Whassamatter with you anyhow? You put on your little sister's shorts this morning by mistake? Go on, get outa here before I smack you myself."

"I'm gonna go find a policeman!"

"Ga-head! But you ain't gonna find one in here, so get lost!"

The kid left, then, making his way out slowly, pausing every other step to kick at the offending earth beneath his feet. He stopped outside the gate to stare hard at Cheo and City Island Pete but they both ignored him. Cheo was actually beginning to feel sorry for the kid, who looked like he was on the verge of tears again.

City Island Pete looked at Cheo. "What's his story?"

"Couldn't find the strike zone," Cheo said.

"Sucks for him," Pete said. "You really hit him?"

"No," Cheo said. "One a his guys did. That he was playing with." Cheo wondered if the kid was really going to go tell his lie to a policeman, and he worried about what kind of trouble that would bring. His mother hated fights, and when you got in one it didn't make much difference to her whether you'd started it or not.

"Nice," Pete said. "You hear 'bout Arturo? He quit."

"How come?" But Cheo was pretty sure he knew the answer to that one.

"I 'ont know. You bring your ball? Wanna throw?"

"Yeah, I guess." He didn't, though, and it was a terrible realization to suddenly know that even something as outstanding as baseball can be ruined by troubles that came limping into your life whether you'd earned them or not.

He slid down off the mailbox anyhow and waited while City Island Pete put on his gear.

Bottom of the third, one out, runners on first and second. Score tied at three, mostly due to City Island Pete. From the mound, Cheo could see the unmarked police car sitting on the overpass just beyond the visitor's bench. A guy who looked a lot like Glass, the cop, leaned against the trunk of the car and watched Cheo try to concentrate on the batter, a little guy who looked like he had no intention of swinging the bat. If Cheo walked him, it would load the bases...

Alcantare was floating around somewhere too, Cheo had noticed him earlier but lost him in the ebb and flow of humanity. And if he was an undercover cop, that's what those guys did, they blended in so you didn't notice them watching you.

Cheo spun the baseball in his hand. This, he thought, must be what the goldfish feels like.

Plus, there had been this woman, he'd spotted her walking up the avenue in between innings, he couldn't be sure but he thought she looked a lot like the one who'd killed her friend Gregory in the basement of his building. He didn't know where she'd gone, either. He put the ball in his glove, wiped his forehead on his sleeve and squinted in at City Island Pete. Pete held his glove open and down low, he was telling Cheo to keep his pitches down. In the field behind him, kids on both teams were yelling. Pete had a fat lip, the previous inning he'd taken a throw from short, blocked home plate and stuck his shoulder into the oncoming base runner, they both went sprawling but Pete came up with blood on his lip and the ball in his mitt. He'd helped the umpire make the right call by jumping around screaming "Out! Out! Out!" Over behind the fence, his mother screamed almost as loud as Pete.

Cheo glanced over his shoulder as the runner took his lead off second base, then he kicked and threw, not his hardest fastball but one he was pretty sure he could get over the plate. The batter's eyes went wide when he sat it floating up there but he let it go by, glanced over at his coach in disgust as the umpire called it.

"Stee-rike one!"

Cheo took the throw back from Pete, watched the opposing coach run through his signs. The batter grimaced and stepped back into the box. His coach isn't letting him swing, Cheo thought, he wants the kid to try for the walk... He looked at both base-runners before he looked in at Pete. He threw it harder this time but it rode high, out of the strike zone. Pete stabbed his mitt up, caught the ball, came up throwing to first. The runner had wandered too far from the bag and he didn't get back in time.

"Out!" The ump and Pete both screamed it together. All over the field the Parkchester Cardinals cheered crazy as the baserunner walked back to the bench, dejected.

Two out, Cheo thought, you might get out of this yet, and City Island Pete was due to bat in their next ups, in the first inning he'd hit a moon shot so far into the weeds beyond the right field fence that no one had been able to find the ball. Cheo made a mental note to go looking for it later...

He ran the count to two and two.

He came set for the next pitch but the kid asked for time and stepped out, stood there staring over at his coach. Cheo kept his eyes on the kid, not the coach, and sure enough it seemed to him that there was a little more purpose in the kid's stance when he stepped back in.

They musta gave him the green light, Cheo thought.

He's gonna swing.

You gotta throw a strike right here, he told himself, if you miss this time the count will be full and you'll wind up walking him for sure, but if you throw another meatball he's gonna be all over it... He stared in at Pete, who was holding down two fingers.

He wanted the curve.

Cheo swallowed, shook his head. No way. Coach would have a pony, right there on the bench.

Pete stared back.

Two fingers.

Cheo's pulse raced as he shrugged mentally, nodded, looked at second, shifted his grip on the ball and then kicked and threw his curve in a real game for the first time. The ball arced high, laces blurring as it spun madly. The batter's arms tried to swing the bat but his knees buckled and his butt tried to grab some dirt, he lost his grip on the bat as the ball spun earthward, bisecting the strike zone neatly as Pete came up out of his crouch to grab it. He'd known it was coming, he was the one who called for it but it had fooled him too... The batter landed on his ass in the dirt. Pete stood yelling exultantly.

The ump stood there with his mouth open.

"Ball three!" he finally said.

"What!?" Everybody yelled it pretty much at the same time, everybody except Coach, who jumped off the bench, his face livid, but he wasn't yelling at the umpire.

He was yelling at Cheo.

Even after the very loud and public ass-chewing was over, it wasn't over. Coach pulled Cheo and City Island Pete out of the game and they went to sit together on the end of the bench, far away from everyone else. From time to time Coach would stand up and yell at them some more. "Who's the coach? Am I still the coach or did someone make one of you the coach without telling me?" He'd sit down, but then a moment later he'd jump back up and do it again: "Did I or did I not say no curve balls?"

And so on.

None of which really required any kind of response.

"Did I not tell you to stay away from those damned buscones?" He was talking about the street agents, adult men of questionable pedigree who would set up shop in city parks and tutor you for twenty-five or thirty bucks an afternoon. Nobody really knew whether they did you any good or not. "Do you think some drunk teaching God only knows what knows better than me? You think he cares about that arm? Huh?"

Cheo wanted to yell back. Did Coach really think Cheo had thirty bucks to spend on some guy running an impromptu baseball clinic? But he knew to keep his mouth shut, as unfair as it seemed. People yelled at him all the time but it was rarely about anything that made any sense to him, and it was even less often that they were interested in anything like a rational discussion about whatever it was that had pissed them off. Basically Coach was mad, he was bigger than you and you were by God gonna do things his way or else. In Cheo's experience, the smart play was to shut up and take it until Coach, or whoever, got tired of him and went off to yell at someone else for a while. That, however, did not make it any easier to sit and watch the Parkchester Cardinals, minus their two best players, lose the game. And the worst of it, maybe, was having Coach mad at him. Coach, the only man in the world he trusted, the first guy who'd ever said anything good about him, who had taken the time and trouble to induct him into the magical world of baseball.

"Yo, Lefty." Cheo was startled to hear the familiar hoarse voice at his ear. He half-turned to see Pelios down on one knee in the dirt right behind the bench. "That was one beautiful curve you snapped off out there. Did you give that kid a case of the jelly-legs or what?"

"The umpire said it was out," Cheo said sourly. "And Coach is pitching a fit."

"He'll get over it," Pelios rasped. "This your catcher? What's your name, kid?"

"That's City Island Pete," Cheo told him.

Pelios nodded to Pete. "That was some dinger you hit. You got a sweet stroke, my brother."

"Thanks." Pete didn't sound happy.

"Anyway," Cheo said, "I can't get the curve to go twelve to six. It always goes like, eleven to five or something."

"Don't worry about it, that's a good thing. Listen, Pete, one thing. Next time you call for the curve, you gotta sell it. Help the umpire see it for a strike, you know what I'm saying? That means you gotta stay down, let the ball come down to you. If you stand up to catch it, the guy will most likely see it high. You stay down, you get the call, because that thing was a strike all the way."

"I know it was," Pete said.

"You gotta be kidding." Cheo said. He pointed in Coach's direction with his chin. "You think there's gonna be a next time? You see what he's like. Next time I throw a curve he'll kill me and Pete both."

"Don't worry about him. He gets tired of losing, you'll be right back in there. Besides, I'll take the rap for it. I'll go tell him that I'm your uncle and I told you to throw it."

"You can't," Cheo said. "You see that guy leaning on the car up on the overpass? He's a cop. His name is Glass, and he wants to get you."

Pelios looked, but without turning his head. "Yeah. Yeah, I see him."

"And there's another one, too, except he don't look like no cop, he looks like a coke dealer. Light skin, long black ponytail. He's gotta be floating around here someplace." Cheo, just that second and almost without any conscious thought, made the decision to side with Pelios and not the policemen. He didn't quite know why. Maybe it was because of the curve, maybe that made them teammates of a sort and you never ratted out a teammate. Anyhow, it had happened and he couldn't back out now. "Plus, there's this lady, she got a couple guys with her, they strangled our super in his apartment the night before last, and then she got mad at one of her guys and stabbed him right in the throat. Left him there dead and bleeding all over the basement floor. Dude's name was Gregory."

"What did she look like?" Pelios' voice seemed even huskier than normal, and very quiet.

"Beautiful," Cheo told him. "White lady, long dark hair. If you seen her, you would stop to look."

"Wow," Pelios said, almost inaudibly. "Well. Damn. I think I know who you mean, and I am real sorry to hear about it." He looked at the avenue behind him, the overpass behind the visitor's bench and the highway in the trench out past the fence. "Well, I'm not gonna lie to you, it looks like they got me boxed in."

"Can you run?" Pete asked him. Cheo felt pretty okay when he heard the question, because it meant Pete was with him.

"Yeah," Pelios said. "But not very far."

"There's a gap in the fence down in the outfield corner," Pete told him. "Go through the hole, follow the path down through the weeds and stuff, you'll come to a tunnel that goes underneath the highway. Trucks use it to get to the junkyards down by the river. You could maybe find a place to hide down in there."

"You know something Pete, you're all right, I don't care what they say about you." He looked around. "Still a tight spot. Listen, boys, I'm gonna leave something with you. Something for safekeeping, like. I don't want it falling into the wrong hands. Don't turn around. It's in a little red envelope. If they get me, they won't get me alive. I want you to go to the cemetery, the name of the place is on the envelope, and the number is on the key, find that mausoleum."

"What' s a mausoleum?" Cheo said.

"It's like a little building with dead people inside, okay? Don't do it unless they get me, now. If they don't, I'll be in touch. Just remember this one thing: The eyes will tell you where to look. You got that?"

"A building with dead people in it?" Pete said, horrified.

"Eyes tell you where to look," Cheo said. "We got it."

"That was one sweet curveball. Watch the game, now."

Cheo's mouth went dry.

After a minute, Glass stood up off the car, said something into a cell phone, then put it in his pocket and started to run. Cheo turned the other way just in time to see Pelios duck through the gap in the fence and break into a lopsided trot.

Coach turned to watch, mouth agape.

A half dozen men separated themselves from the crowds either watching the game or drifting by on the sidewalk and joined in the chase.

A small red envelope, maybe an inch and a half by two inches, rested in the dirt behind the bench, Cheo did not even have to bend down to scoop it up and tuck it into his back pocket. He and City Island Pete looked at each other. "Let's get outa here," Pete said. "While they're all chasing him."

The first gunshots came about thirty seconds later, and then everybody was leaving.

CHAPTER 6

Sunday morning early was Cheo's second favorite time of the week, particularly in the summer when it got light while almost everyone was still in bed. Cheo's mother would give him a twenty and he would walk the four eerily silent blocks to Ellie's Diner where he would buy two everything bagels with lox spread, a large black coffee with three sugars and a Sunday New York Daily News for his mother and a cinnamon-raisin bagel with butter for himself. To carry it all home was one of the best feelings he knew, even if it was beyond his comprehension how anyone could actually ask for anything as disgustingly horrible as an everything bagel, which got rolled in little bits of onion, salt, garlic and God only knew what else before it got put in the oven, and if one crumb of that gack got stuck to his cinnamon-raisin it could ruin the whole thing, but that was what she wanted, so what could you do.

The Black Hand Crew was nowhere in evidence when he passed by that morning. Maybe they were still in bed. Still, most Sundays they had at least a token presence on the corner so Cheo figured that the gang members were keeping their heads down. The Black Hand, like most enterprises of its kind, had been a careful and fragile balance of greed and fear. Pelios had kicked it all out of whack, and Death, perhaps weary of waiting for Cheo, would probably snack on a few of the more unfortunate members of the gang before balance was restored. There might even be an article in the paper he carried, a picture of a weeping mother, with a smaller inset showing a face not much older than Cheo's, and the all-too familiar story line, another young man shot execution style, no suspects, and would any members of the public who'd seen it happen please call...

"Lefty! Psst! Yo, Lefty!"

It was City Island Pete. He was hiding under a stoop behind some trash cans.

The two boys walked slowly in the direction of Valentine Street. "Do you think he's dead?" Pete said. "That guy from the game yesterday, with the limp."

Cheo hated to think it might be true. "Maybe," he said. "I don't know. Because they were all running after him and he wasn't moving that fast. And some of them were shooting. But the dude is way smooth..."

"He said we should use the key," Pete said. "You know, if something happened to him."

"I know."

"There were cops at my house this morning," Pete said. "My mom pitched a fit."

"Why?"

Pete shrugged. "You know, the way they talk to you. When they see her blue hair, right, they figure she's wack."

"I ain't saying nothing," Cheo said.

"I know, I know," Pete said. "She is wack, a little bit. But anyhow she was arguing and yelling so they made her go with them to make a statement. I was supposed to go over to my cousin's house but I took the bus down here instead."

They were about a half a block from Valentine. "Wait up," Cheo said, and the two of them took refuge in a doorway.

Pete stuck his head out and peered down toward the intersection. "Where are them guys at, the ones that work on your corner?" he said, wary.

"The Black Hand Crew," Cheo said. "They was hassling me and Arturo, and Pelios messed them up. I mean, he messed them up good. Now none of them is as bad as he used to be. I think they're all trying to figure out which one of them is the big dog that the rest of them all need to be afraid of."

"Pelios messed them up? He's the guy with the limp."

"Yeah."

"There's a guy down there, he's sitting in the front seat of a gypsy cab. White dude, I think he's got a pony tail."

Cheo changed places with Pete, stuck his head out for a look. "I think that's Alcantare," he said. "He's one of the cops that came to my house the other day. Him and his partner are the ones after Pelios."

"How come they want Pelios?"

"Peanut butter," Cheo said. "Scootch down, he's turning the car around." They both ducked down low. Cheo could still see, though, as the gypsy cab stopped right in front of the doorway to Cheo's building, and Glass came out, escorting Cheo's mother. He put her in the back of the car. Cheo pushed on the outer door of the building behind him. It was open. "In here," he told Pete. "Until they go by."

Pete followed him inside. "Peanut butter?"

"Long story." Cheo turned and looked at his catcher. City Island Pete was waiting for Cheo to trust him. "You remember the last series with the Angels?" Cheo asked him.

Pete nodded. "We lost three out of four."

"Game four, okay, I was listening on my radio, right, and I look out my bedroom window and I see this guy, he's limping up the block..."

Pete listened to the whole story without interrupting, but when Cheo was done, he had some questions. "Those two cops," he said. "Alcantare and the other guy. You don't like 'em."

"No."

"Why not?"

"Because they're not from here. They're from Queens."

"So what?"

"So how come they're not down in Queens chasing Queens bad

guys? How come they gotta come up here to our neighborhood? They wanna get Pelios, that's what they said, but they can't even arrest him because he ain't done nothing wrong since he got out of jail. That's what they told my moms. Don't they got any criminals down in Queens? Guys that have already done something to get arrested for? They're up here looking for peanut butter, just like all the rest of them."

"So you trust Pelios."

Cheo took a moment to consider before answering. "Not exactly. Anyhow, we don't even know if he's still alive."

"What if he is?"

"I don't know, man. I mean, he taught me the curve, you know what I'm saying?"

"You're trusting him behind him showing you how to throw a curve ball."

That did sound pretty stupid... "No. I don't think so. Maybe. I don't know, man, how many guys have ever stopped to teach you something? Who taught you how to catch?"

"Coach," Pete said, and Cheo could tell that Pete was still stinging from Coach pulling the two of them out of the game and sitting them on the bench, even if the game did wind up getting called on account of gunfire.

"Besides Coach."

Pete shook his head. "Nope. I mean, except for Pelios. You heard him, it was my fault your curve got called high. I'm sorry, Lefty, but I thought it was gonna be way high, especially at first! I thought you was gonna bean that kid! And he thought so too, you see him bailing out of that batter's box? But then the ball broke down and right over the plate, I hadda reach back down to catch it. Pelios was right, it was my fault the ump called it high. Coach would'na benched us if you'da struck that kid out."

"It ain't your fault," Cheo said, "because you didn't know. Now you do. Next time you cost me a strike, me and Coach will take turns yelling at you."

"You think he's gonna cut us? I never seen him so mad..."

"And let us go play for someone else? No way."

Pete thought about that for a minute, then he went back to his original question. "So you think Pelios was telling the truth."

Cheo had his answer ready this time. "No. I think he was playing everybody. The Black Hand Crew, that drunk of a super, the Greeks, the cops, me, he was playing us all, but they musta killed him, that's why they coming after us so hard. That's how come they picked up your moms, and mine. Me and you are all they got left."

"My mom can't tell them squat, cause she don't know anything. And she probably wouldn't, anyhow." He left the obvious question unasked. What would Cheo's mother tell them? How much, for that matter, had Cheo told her? He'd shown her the key, she'd held it in one quivering hand before handing it back to him and telling him to put it in his pocket and keep his donut hole shut until Pelios came back for it. Had she had the time or the inclination to read the name on the envelope? Would she remember it?

"We gotta get there before they do," Cheo said. "Let's go."

CHAPTER 7

I t all looked so overwhelming from the platform, which was a flat concrete slab elevated high above the street where Cheo and City Island Pete waited for the number six train. As far as Cheo could see, buildings covered the hard dirt of The Bronx, mile after mile of it. He did not want to admit that he was afraid, not even to himself, so he stood at the railing staring out over the undulating rooftops, feeling slightly seasick. He knew his own little neighborhood, knew it intimately, but the remainder of the vast, twisted tangle of streets and buildings that was The Bronx stretched away back out of sight, as unknown and strange as some foreign country on the far side of the world. And that was just this one borough, there were four more beyond, not to mention upstate and Long Island and Jersey and God only knew what else. He glanced over at Pete, who was squinting up at the big subway map, and for a second Cheo considered suggesting that they abandon this adventure, just go home, surrender the key Pelios had given them to the first person who came asking for it.

"I got four trips left on my Metrocard," Pete said. "I think we gotta ride the six into Manhattan, then change for the L at Union Square."

"I'll pay you back," Cheo told him.

"Are you kidding?" Pete said. "Once we get to the cemetery and find the money, you can buy me my own car. I want a Buick, a big one, so big you can't even park it anywhere, with the windows all blacked out so nobody can see me."

Cheo had no problem spending Pelios' as yet largely theoretical money. "We find anything, we split it fifty-fifty," he said. "You can buy your own car. And your own parking spot."

Pete scowled. "I'd have to hire somebody to guard my spot. Keep all the other cars from taking it."

"You see?" Cheo told him. "You ain't even rich yet, already you got problems."

Pete came over to stand next to Cheo at the rail. "What would you do if we found a million bucks? What would you buy first?"

"I 'on't know," Cheo said.

Pete grinned. "I know you. You'd get box seats at the stadium."

Eighty-one home games, plus the post-season... It was too much for him to imagine. Would going to that many games mean he'd have to give up on the Parkchester Cardinals? "Maybe," he said doubtfully.

"A new glove, then."

"No way." Cheo's baseball glove had been donated to him through a Yankee's outreach program and he was keeping it forever. Besides, he was superstitious about such things. Why change something that was working for you? Who knew how well, or even if a new one would work? What if a new glove turned him into a stumble-footed, error-prone embarrassment? "No way."

"You can't think of anything, can you?" His friend Pete was laughing at him. "You see? That's why you need a girlfriend. She'll help you spend your money."

Cheo had to grin in spite of his mood.

"That's so wack," Pete said. "What's the thing you want most in the world? Don't think about it, say it quick."

Cheo felt small, diminished by the scope of the view from the platform. "To be on the team," he said. "To play good at short. Get some hits." He paused. "Throw a mean curve."

"I guess money ain't gonna help you." All the mirth drained out of Pete's face. "That last one you tossed was a real mother. And it was my fault it wasn't a strike."

Not that again, Cheo thought. "No, it..."

Pete cut him off. "Yeah it was. Because I stood up to get it when I didn't need to. It will never happen again. I swear it."

"Forget it," Cheo told him. "Besides, you heard what Coach said. He's never gonna let me throw another curve."

"Oh, please," Pete said, obviously doubtful of Coach's ability to maintain his convictions in the face of such a beautiful pitch. "So anyway, getting in a game is the best thing you can think of. What's the worst?"

"Sitting on the bench," Cheo said promptly. "Watching everybody else play."

"Dude, you gotta get out more," Pete told him. "There's more to life than baseball."

"I can't help it," Cheo said. "Listen, how much trouble are we gonna get you into, doing this?"

"My mom has a blue mohawk," Pete said, like that answered everything.

"So what?"

Pete shook his head over Cheo's lack of insight. "Dude. She might get mad but she won't stay mad, not if there's a good story to tell when it's all over. Anyway, what about you? They put your moms in a cop car, man, she's gonna freak."

"Maybe. I'll call her later. Tell her not to worry."

"How you gonna do that? You ain't got no cell phone."

Cheo reached into his pocket and fished out the one that Glass and Alcantare had given him. "Those cops gave me this. I'm supposed to keep it with me wherever I go. I can use it to call her later." He handed it to Pete.

Pete looked at the phone. "These things only work when you turn 'em on, you know," he said, and he held a button down. A few seconds later the phone lit up and he gave it back.

Cheo stuck the phone back in his pocket. "You know what? I think we're supposed to do this. You know what I'm saying?"

"I guess," Pete said. "Because of your buddy Pelios."

Cheo, not quite sure if Pelios had been his friend or not, nodded his head.

"You think he's dead?" Pete said. "You think they got him?"

Cheo could feel the little red envelope, which he had tucked in his sneaker for safekeeping. "He didn't come to get his key back."

"No," Pete said. "So I guess it's on you and me."

There was a train coming, Cheo felt it before he could actually see it, the rails creaked, complaining about something very heavy and distant moving steadily closer. A White guy struggled up the steps of the platform on the other side of the tracks, opposite from where Cheo and Pete waited. He was tall, thin, and completely bald, bent over, he had a hawkish look on his face and he grimaced as he walked, as though each step caused him pain. He wore a tattered pair of jeans, black tie shoes with no socks, and instead of a shirt he had on what looked like an old bathrobe with sleeves that didn't quite reach his elbows. It flapped open, revealing a bare chest covered with tattoos that made that part of him look like a garage door covered with graffiti. He crabbed up to the edge of the platform and peered in the direction of the approaching train, then turned and scowled at Cheo with eyes that didn't point in quite the same direction.

Cheo felt his skin crawl. "Yo, Pete, check this guy. He's creeping me out."

Pete looked over at the guy, but the guy had turned and was hobbling down the platform. "What?" Pete said. "He ain't nothing but some homeless dude. Just a bum."

"I guess," Cheo said. At least there was no way the guy could be Alcantare in one of his disguises. "I'm glad he's going the other way."

"He ain't going nowhere," Pete said. "He's just gonna ride the trains the way those guys do. Besides, that's our train, it's gotta go like two more stops until it reaches the end of the line, and then it turns around and comes back this way."

"Oh great," Cheo said, staring down the tracks at the train. It seemed like it was inching along, like you could walk faster than it moved.

"What could you do?" Pete said. "Besides, we're lucky. We miss this one, we'd hafta sit here and wait like a hour for the next one." The train pulled into the station, shrieking and squealing as it braked to a stop.

The doors groaned open, and then a moment later they slammed shut again and then the train jerked into forward motion and pulled out to continue on its unhurried journey. Cheo looked for the guy in the bathrobe, but he was gone.

A few more travelers straggled up to Cheo and Pete's side of the station to wait. Pete went into subway mode: expressionless face, no eye contact, a general appearance that suggested he might not be fully conscious. Cheo did his best to copy the look but he was more paranoid than his friend and no one moved anywhere in his line of sight without him taking note.

The train eventually came back, just like Pete said it would. It seemed to Cheo that they'd been waiting for it half the day, but it had really only been a half hour or so. They got on, Cheo looked around for the bathrobe guy but he didn't see him. The car they were in had a wino of its own, though, an amazingly fragrant White guy with white hair and a beard who sat in the far corner. He slumped forward, almost lost in his heavy gray overcoat, his head on his knees. The doors closed, the train lurched into motion, and Cheo was reminded of what he'd learned in school about inertia, bodies at rest tending to remain at rest and all that because the sudden forward motion almost knocked the old wino out of his seat. He saved himself at the last moment, though, he came out of his funk long enough to grab onto the pole next to his seat, but then he phased back out again.

Pete paid no attention to the old man, he was sneaking a look at a girl sitting across the aisle from them, she had dark hair with two tiny red streaks in the front, she looked like she'd just stepped out of a magazine. She was too old for Pete, she had to be sixteen or eighteen and she ignored them both, stared regally off into space. Cheo did the same thing, he got into it after a few minutes, pretended he was the only guy in the car, the only guy on the whole train, even. From the car windows he couldn't see the tracks the train rode on, couldn't see most of the buildings, just the bigger ones that stuck up here and there into the empty sky. It was an odd sensation, to float along across the top of everything, with only the clattering racket of the subway car to remind him he was still tied on, still stuck to the surface of the planet. He wondered what it would be like to ride on a real sailing ship, where you could look out and see nothing but the vast ocean, and for a second he thought how cool it would be if his life ever took him that far...

Pete tugged at his sleeve. "Your buddy," Pete said. "He's in the next car."

"The bathrobe dude? You gotta be kidding me. What's he doing?"

Pete shrugged. "Who knows?"

Cheo leaned forward in his seat and peered through the door windows into the adjoining car but he couldn't see the guy. Don't sweat it, he told himself. There are other people here, so nothing will happen, probably.

The train they were on was a local, meaning it stopped every few minutes to let people on or off, in this case, mostly on. Pete ignored them all and they ignored him, and Cheo tried to follow along.

The train made its last stop in The Bronx at Third Avenue, and once it left that station it picked up speed and made a screeching left-hand turn, jerking the car violently back and forth. This time the old wino was thrown completely out of his seat and he rolled down the center of the car, bouncing off legs, poles and benches like a pinball. The doors between the cars opened, filled the car with a rush of wind and sound until it slammed shut again, and the bathrobe guy strode down the aisle. "Brothers and sisters," he shouted, reproachful. "Brothers and sisters! As ye have done to the least of these, my brothers..." He reached the old wino, cradled the half-conscious man in his arms and lifted him to his feet. A half-pint of Fleishman's slipped out of one of the old man's pockets and the bathrobe guy scooped it up and shoved it back where it came from. He glared at a young man who occupied a seat nearby. "Un-ass that chair, boy, you hear me? If you know what's good for you..."

The guy looked, for a second, like he wanted to fight, but then he moved, and so did the lady next to him. The bathrobe guy settled the old wino in the seat, sat down next to him. "It's all right, my brother," he said, and then he glanced over at Cheo out of the corner of his eye.

Cheo's guts had turned to ice but he didn't show it, he glared back, his face hard as the train dove into the tunnel that would take them under the river. It felt, for a moment, like he was trapped underground. Don't be stupid, Cheo told himself, when the train is between stations you got nowhere to run either way... Funny, though, the way the guy looked at you, with one eye off-kilter.

The bathrobe guy got to his feet, grimacing. He fished a battered styrofoam coffee cup out of a pocket and made his way to the end of the car and started pan-handling. Cheo watched him as he made his way through the car. Someone put a buck in his cup. "God bless you, sister," the guy said. "God bless you. May you become a mighty nation."

That should teach you, Cheo told her silently. Give the dude money, now you got to listen to his bull... Pete tugged at Cheo's sleeve. "Get ready," he whispered. "When we get to the next big station, we're gonna run. We gotta lose this guy."

"When is that?" Cheo whispered back.

"I don't know. Just be ready."

The bathrobe guy made his way back up through the car, tilling the flinty Bronx soil but finding no more budding saints. He passed by Cheo and Pete, shaking his cup, but he didn't stop. When he got to the end of the car he looked back at the old wino, then at Cheo, then he stuck the cup back in his pocket and opened the door and made his way into the next car.

"What the hell," Pete said. "What is it with you and these nut jobs? You gotta start wearing a different shirt or something."

"It ain't the shirt," Cheo said. "It's the key." He felt it pressing up against the sole of his foot. "He knows I got it."

"How could he know that? You been watching too many movies."

"No way," Cheo said. "Pelios did this on purpose. He knew. That's why he came to The Bronx, because he knew all these rats were gonna come looking for him."

"And he was gonna get them? When they came after him, he was gonna take them out? But instead, they got him first. So now what?"

"We could turn back," Cheo said. "Go home. Give up the key to the cops."

"Pelios gave it to us," Pete said, looking stubborn. "Screw them guys."

"Do you remember the name on the envelope?"

"Cavalry," Pete said.

"No, that's horses, dummy. Cal-vary."

"Big deal."

"Just don't forget it. And the number on the key is 870."

"Whassamatter, you planning on losing the key?"

"No," Cheo said. "But if anything happens to me, you could still get there ahead of them and get the money first. If there really is any money there."

"'If?' What do you mean, 'if?' Do you think Pelios was lying?"

Cheo thought about it. "No," he finally said.

"Why not?"

"Because you probably ain't gonna catch many rats with pretend peanut butter. You got to have the real thing."

The car started to get crowded, by now all the seats were taken except the one next to the old wino, and people were standing, holding on to the poles. Cheo peered past Pete through the windows into the next car but there was still no sign of the bathrobe guy. He leaned over and whispered in Pete's ear. "I don't think we need to run. Let's just mix in when everybody gets off."

Pete nodded. "Okay, but keep an eye out. If that guy is really following us, he's gonna be watching."

"I don't see him," Cheo said.

"Me neither," Pete said. "Just be ready." The subway map was on the wall behind his head, and Pete contorted himself in his seat to read it. "The next stop," he said, turning back around, "is Lex. I think we should get off, it looks like we can change for the Q there."

"Got you," Cheo said.

It seemed easy at first, a lot of people were exiting the train and Cheo and Pete were in the middle of the crowd. Everyone shuffled along the platform, more or less in order, heading for the same set of stairs. The two boys were halfway up the first flight when they heard shouting down on the platform they'd just left. Cheo saw the woman first, her dark hair flying as she ran, and then the guys, the men who'd been with her the night she'd killed the super in the basement of his building on Valentine. He whacked Pete on the back. "Run," he said, and he and Pete took off, slithering their way through the thicket of larger bodies crowded together on the stairs.

More shouting voices began to add to the din as commuters on the platform behind them began objecting to being shoved aside. Cheo and Pete, who didn't have to shove anyone, paused at the top of the stairs where they were presented with a choice: there was a second set of stairs that led up out of the station and onto Lexington Avenue, and the other way there was a long white-tiled hallway. The sign over the entrance to the hallway claimed it was how you got to the Q platform. They took the hallway, mostly because they'd already talked about the Q, and besides, there was no time for further discussion.

The hallway was almost empty, and Cheo and Pete's footsteps echoed loudly as they ran for all they were worth. It seemed like an absurdly long hallway, but maybe it only felt that way when someone was chasing you. They were almost to the end when they heard shouts behind them. Cheo didn't want to look back, he was too afraid of what he might see. Instead, he ran harder than ever, taking some comfort in the fact that Pete was able to keep pace.

The reached the end of the hallway and suddenly they were on another subway platform. Most of the people who were standing around waiting for the train ignored the two of them, but a few turned to look. "Let's keep going," Cheo told Pete. "We need to find a place to hide."

"Where?" Pete said, looking around.

Cheo saw a door farther down the platform. "This way," he said.

"Dude! The men's room? Do you know how disgusting..."

"Come on, quick! Maybe they won't look in there."

They went in, breathing hard.

The smell in the room was almost like a physical presence, it was almost as though circus animals had been using the place instead of men. From inside the door you could see a row of toilet stalls without any doors and a couple without any toilets, just a hole in the floor. Across from them were some broken sinks. Pete, reluctant to enter further into the room, paused by the door but he came all the way in when he heard noises on the platform outside.

There was a guy in the last stall.

He wasn't actually inside the stall, but rather, standing in the opening. He looked like your basic businessman on his way to the office, he wore the usual suit and tie but his pants and his boxers weren't in the usual place, they were down around his knees. He stood there with his back to Cheo and Pete, he didn't seem to notice them at first but the entrance door, by opening and then closing behind the two boys, must have created eddies in the stench that hung in the room like smoke, and sensing the disturbance, the guy turned and looked over his shoulder without moving anything but his head.

"Unh," he said, but then he focused on Cheo and Pete. "Geddadda-here!" he snarled. "G'wan! Get out!"

Cheo steadied Pete with a hand to his back. "No way!" he said, trying not to yell. "Who the hell are you? You get out!"

The guy's face flushed a deep red. "Goddammit! Geddadda... Never mind," he said, and he shook himself. "I'm outa here." He took a half step out of the stall but kept his back to Cheo and Pete while he struggled with his trousers. Cheo and Pete retreated to a corner as the guy made for the door, looking like he'd gotten dressed in a real hurry that morning, or was maybe trying to smuggle a ferret in his pants. Cheo breathed a sigh of relief when the door closed behind the guy but it caught in his throat when he realized that the man hadn't been alone in the last booth. A muscular White guy wearing a tight tee shirt, loose khaki shorts and an Army haircut stepped out, his face contorted and red. "You just cost me twenty bucks," he hissed, and he took a step closer. "You little bastards don't belong in here, and if you don't leave right now I'm gonna show you why."

Cheo heard voices on the platform outside. "Mister," he said, trying to keep his voice down. "We can't go. There's people outside looking for us. They wanna kill us!"

"Choose your poison," the guy hissed. "You stay here and I'll kill you."

Cheo could feel Pete quaking and he wasn't far from panic himself. "Please, mister, we don't wanna bother nobody, but..."

Just then the door behind him began opening slowly until the bathrobe guy from the train edged his way into the room. Seeing Cheo and Pete, he held a finger up to his lips as the door swung shut again. "She's out there," he whispered. "She got two more with her, and if she finds us, we don't stand a chance."

"Who is she?" Cheo asked.

"Who is 'we'?" Pete said, under his breath.

"Satan's baby sister," the guy said, and then the man in the shorts, his face almost purple, charged the bathrobe guy with his hands raised. The bathrobe guy whirled and a second later he had the man in the shorts down on the disgusting floor, his hands around the guy's throat. "You are an abomination," he growled, his face inches from the other man. "I swore a solemn oath not to shed another man's blood, but I don't think you count..."

The guy on the floor made a horrible retching sound.

"Hey buddy," Pete said softly. "Don't hurt him. He ain't done nothing to you."

The bathrobe guy thought about it for a moment, then eased up. "The kid just saved your life," he said. The guy in the shorts made rattling sounds as he tried to force air back into his lungs. "You go crawl back into your hole and say a prayer of thanks to the sweet lord Jesus. A silent one. You make one more sound and I swear by God I'll strangle you with your own guts, kid or no kid."

The guy scuttled across the floor, retching.

The bathrobe guy turned and looked at Cheo, who read the big tattoo across the guy's chest. "Jesus," he said, pronouncing it 'Hay-soos,' the Spanish way. "Is that you?"

The man shook his head. "Our lord and savior," he said, and he pointed to another name, in much smaller print down closer to his waistline. 'Dzekas,' it said.

The noise of the man's crying filled the bathroom. Cheo could not think of a more shameful sound.

"Yo! Over there in the stall!" Dzekas snarled.

The guy in the stall managed to strangle his sobs.

"You knock off that noise or by God I swear I'll cut your throat. Do you hear me?"

A squeak served for the answer.

Dzekas turned back to the door, opened it a crack and peered out. "I don't see none of them coming yet," he said.

Cheo sucked in a big breath. "So who are you, really?"

Dzekas looked away from the crack in the door, over at Cheo. "I was one of them."

Cheo was shocked. "One of..."

"One of the Greeks. So was Pelios. That woman you seen out on the subway platform, her name is Tasya Gaitanis. Or it is now, anyway. She took the old man's family name, she wouldn'a had the guts to do that if the old man was still alive. Me and Pelios, we used to work for the guy. Her father, old man Gaitanis."

"You were gangsters," Pete said, awed.

"Some would say that," Dzekas said, quiet. "And maybe they'd have a right. But we didn't have a name for what we was, or what we done. Hell, I wasn't much older than you two when I first went to work for him."

"What did you do?" Cheo asked him. "What was your job?"

Dzekas swallowed and peered back out through the crack in the door. "Whatever he told me," he said, without looking at them. "See, you might be a good guy, but if you're in a bad place, sometimes you got to do what you have to do to get by. But those things you do, after a while they can turn you all black inside. You take old man Gaitanis, he was a great guy. Give you the shirt off his back. Pay your doctor bills when you got sick. Give you a job, get you a place to live. Even find you some congenial companionship, you know what I'm saying, if he thought you needed it. He was a good man to work for, long as you didn't get on his bad side. He could be a good man when he wanted to, like I said, but he had some evil in him. Once I seen him chop off a guy's toes, all of them, one at a time, and then half his fingers just because he thought the guy was lying to him." He glanced back at Cheo and Pete. "Let's just put it this way: he sent a lot of men to Perdition. Women too, more than once."

"What's perdition?" Cheo said. Pete caught his eye, drew a finger across his throat. "Oh," Cheo said. "So what happened to him?"

"Gaitanis? One hot summer night," Dzekas said, "probably right about the time you guys were born, the devil come for him. Old Patch caught up with Gaitanis in Douglaston, Queens, in a building the old man owned out there. Patch told him, 'Costas, you done all the evil you're gonna do, you spilled all the blood you're gonna spill, your time has come.' And they found the old man's body there on the floor with a bullet hole right between his eyes."

"Okay," Cheo said, "so maybe the devil got him, but I bet somebody else hadda pull the trigger. Who was that?"

"Well that, my young friend, is still a unanswered question. The cops grabbed Pelios that night, and they put him away for manslaughter. But I never believed Pelios done it. Not that he wasn't capable, mind you, but him and the old man, they was tight. They was just like father and son. And when they put him on trial, he stood there like a marble statue and listened to all the things they accused him of and he never said a word. Kept his trap shut. And there's plenty he coulda said, too, half the guys in Astoria was shittin' a pickle worrying about what he was gonna tell the cops to try to get himself out of going to jail. But he never done it, he never gave up a one of us. Nobody believed it at first, but after he went off to prison and nothing else happened, he was a hero, believe you me. For a while.

"For a while.

"What happened, though, nobody could find the old man's money. Oh, there was a little bit here and a little bit there, but nothing like what we all knew he had. Tasya turned some up, but not a lot. Under a million. Price of a nice house, say. So there has to be millions out there somewhere, salted away, but nobody could find it. Drove us all crazy. Anyway, after a while, people started saying, 'Pelios, that son of a bitch, he musta done it just like the cops said he did, he musta killed the old man and hid his dough,' him being the old man's driver and whatnot. That's what everybody said. We all put a big circle around his release date, you know what I'm saying."

"Still," Cheo said. "If Pelios didn't kill the old guy, who did?"

Dzekas stared out out at the subway platform. "I'll tell you what I think happened," he finally said. "See, you gotta understand, Pelios comes from a different time. A previous administration, you might say, and you gotta remember that when you're trying to figure out what he's thinking. Guys nowadays, they get arrested, okay, they're singing La Boheme before the cops get the cuffs on, almost. Everybody wants to be gangsta but nobody wants to go to jail. They can't wait to sell out alla their friends so as to stay out of trouble. Pelios, he was never like that. I never thought he wanted to be gangsta to begin with, he just wound up with us because he didn't have no place else to go. When he was eighteen, okay, he's driving the old man out to see his girlfriend, car had a tail light out or something. Something stupid like that. Long story short, they get pulled over, the cops find a pistol under the driver's seat. Pelios takes one look at Gaitanis, tells the cops, 'Hey, it's my gun.' He winds up doing a year and a half upstate." Dzekas looked at the two boys. "But I tell you what, I know the kid didn't have no gun. But the old man, he was known to carry a piece now and then, up until that time you couldn't tell him no different, he thought he was Superman and nobody could touch him."

"So if it wasn't his gun," Pete said, "then how come..."

"How come he went away for it? That's what I'm trying to tell you. He's old school. The old man was the boss, Pelios worked for him, took the man's money, so he stepped up and took the fall. Of course, nobody said nothing, but that's the way it was. Old man treated him like a hero after he got out. Threw him a big party. Pelios walks through the door, right, Gaitanis jumps up, yells 'My son!' as loud as he can, like he's Moses or something. Did Moses have any kids? Maybe it was one of those other guys, Abraham or whatever, but you catch my drift."

"Well, if he didn't shoot Gaitanis, who did?"

"I'm getting to that. See, there's a long list of guys who wouldn't have minded putting Costas cold in the ground, and a couple of women, too. Gaitanis had some enemies, you can believe that. But the person who hated him the most was his daughter."

Cheo scowled at Dzekas. "What'd he do to her?"

"Well, I don't quite know how to explain that to a couple of upstanding young gents such as yourselves, who ain't done nobody dirty in their whole lives, yet." He fell silent for a moment or two, considering. "Okay, see, Costas already had a wife and son, lived right there in his house in Astoria. No daughter. But he had a girlfriend, too, you know what I mean, and she wasn't no spring chicken herself on account of they were together for such a long time. And she lived in that apartment building in Douglaston, which Gaitanis owned, which they found him dead inside of, with a bullet in his head. And she had a daughter, girl was about seventeen at the time."

"She was his daughter?" Pete said. "He was her father?"

"Ah well, you know, who could say for sure? She didn't look much like him but she was just about as mean as he was. Way better looking, though. And he wasn't no kind of father, not to her, not to his son neither, matter of fact, but he wouldn't give the girl the sweat off his, ah, you know, brow. Walked away and let her raise her own self. You know what I mean?"

"Yeah." Cheo and Pete both said it together.

"So anyhow, we all figured she was his. Because for a buck she'd cut your liver out with her nail file and for another dollar she'd cook it and eat it."

"She don't need a nail file," Cheo said. "She carries a little silver knife."

"That's her," Pete said, going pale. "Out there someplace, looking for us." He pointed out through the bathroom door. "You think she did it."

Dzekas shrugged. "Well, I wouldn't bet my life on it, but if I was a cop and it was my job to find out, she'da been doing the hot squats, I can promise you that. But the point of all this is, Pelios was in love with her. And last time I seen him, he sounded like he still was."

"You're kidding me." Cheo sounded disgusted.

"Not a bit. Mad, crazy, out of his mind, fall down on his knees in love."

"So you think she capped her own father, and then Pelios took the fall for her," Cheo said.

"Bingo," Dzekas said. "Now, in regards to our present predicament, there's two things you got to remember. One, prison changes you. It ages you something terrible. Turns you into somebody your mother wouldn't recognize. That first time, before he went away for the gun, he maybe coulda been almost anything he put his mind to. Coulda been a lawyer or a doctor, coulda went into business, he was plenty smart enough. Coulda played quarterback for the Giants, maybe. The Jets, for sure. But when he come out a year and a half later, he might of looked twenty-one but inside he was closer to fifty. He didn't have no future, not like before. The world was a smaller place. Alls he could be was what he already was."

"A bad guy," Pete said.

"You could say that. And when he went away the second time, he did twelve years. Imagine what he's got left now." Dzekas shook his head. "You wanna be something, you know what I'm saying, you want a shot at being regular, you gotta stay outa jail, I don't give a damn how smart you are."

"What's the other thing we need to remember?"

"He's still nuts for Tasya," Dzekas said. "He still can't think right about her. He's still waiting for her to love him back."

"Sounds like he's got a long wait," Pete said.

"Yeah, you might know that, and I know it for sure, but you can't talk to a guy when he's in that condition. He hasta find out for himself. Some guys never find out." He peered out through the crack in the door again. "They're coming. We still got a minute or two." He turned, looked over his shoulder in the direction of the bathroom's other occupant. Then he turned his hawkish glare at Cheo and Pete, held a finger up to his lips.

Cheo and Pete both nodded.

Dzekas walked swiftly to the rearmost stall. "I'm gonna say this to you one last time," he snarled at the guy in the stall. "You make one goddam sound and I swear by all that's holy I will cut your tongue out. I will have it in my pocket when I leave here, I don't give a damn what else happens. You understand me?"

The man's response was understandably silent but apparently Dzekas was satisfied with it because he turned his back on the stall and made his way back to the bathroom doorway. He opened the door again, just the tiniest of cracks, and looked out. He glanced once at Cheo and Pete. "Listen, guys, I don't know whether or not they'll look in here, but I'm gonna brace myself against the door anyhow, just in case. Okay? So don't make a peep. Everybody stays quiet, pray Jesus the good Lord willing we'll sneak through this all in okay shape. Got it?"

"Yeah," Pete said.

Cheo was confused. "If all that stuff you said is true," he said, trying to keep his voice down, "What the hell are you doing in here with us?"

Dzekas bared his teeth in a crocodile smile. "Hell is the word, my brother. 'Though your sins be as scarlet,' the good book says so and mine are redder than a baboon's ass but Jesus loves me all the same. Quiet now, I promise you I'll tell you everything just as soon as we get clear of this goddam sewer."

Someone came and rattled the doorknob a few minutes later but the door might as well have been bolted shut, Dzekas had his entire body jammed up against it. Five more minutes passed, Dzekas had veins popping out on his neck before he finally eased off the pressure. He cracked the door open and peered out. "Don't see nobody looking," he said. "My brothers. Beware of Greeks bearing gifts. Anybody give one of you two something in the last week or so?"

"Pelios," Cheo said. Pete looked at him in horror.

Dzekas' eyes narrowed when he heard the name. "You seen him, then. And what did he give you?"

"Curve ball," Cheo said.

Dzekas exhaled, and so did Pete. "Well I'm sure that was very kind of him, but I had in mind something of a more temporal nature, something you might hold in your hands, like, say, a pair of sneakers."

"The phone," Pete said.

"Oh, yeah," Cheo said, and he pulled it out.

"Pelios gave you this?"

"No," Cheo said. "The cops."

Dzekas took it, flipped it open, then turned it over and popped the battery off. "Okay," he said, relieved. "That's how they're doing it."

"Doing what?"

"Following you." He showed the two of them the phone, still missing its battery. There was a white strip stuck to the inside, underneath where the battery went. "That white thing right there is some kind of a beacon. Bet on it."

"Flush it down the toilet," Cheo said.

"That's one option," Dzekas said. "But I think we might be better served if I was to go slip it into someone else's pocket. Someone waiting for a Bronx-bound train, say. But I don't want to leave you two in here with that..." He took a step in the direction of the man in the stall.

"Noo..." Pete said. "Leave him alone. Come on, man, he stayed quiet, like you said."

Dzekas stood suspended between murder and mercy. "So be it," he finally said. "I s'pose the bastard's recompense is the good Lord's business and none of my own anyhow. Let's go."

CHAPTER 8

Another train rattled into the station as the three of them made their way down the platform. After it departed, all of the people who'd gotten off took the stairs up and out. Dzekas led Cheo and Pete down to the very end of the platform, where they vaulted a small gate and went down some blackened stairs and a few yards into the darkness of the tunnel. There was a small alcove there with room enough for the two boys to stand. "You guys okay here?" Dzekas said.

"Yeah," Cheo said.

"Good. Don't move, now, and don't touch nothing. There might be another train along before I get back, this might take a few minutes, but if you stand still you won't get squished. Or 'lectrocuted. Okay?"

"Yeah. Does that lady chasing after us know who you are? If she sees you, will she recognize you?"

"Not a chance," Dzekas said.

"How come?"

"Because when the good Lord changed my heart, he changed my face, too. Be cool, my brothers, and I'll be right back."

They watched him go. "We gonna run?" Cheo asked Pete.

"I dunno. What do you think?"

"I think the guy is wack."

"Yeah, me, too. But..."

"Yeah, I know what you mean. He might be crazy but I think he's for real. Did you see his face when I said Pelios' name?"

"Yeah," Pete said, sounding shaky. "I thought you was gonna tell him about the key. I tell you what, let's wait for him to come back, okay, and we'll listen to the rest of his story. We can always take off later if we have to. I mean, he sure took care of that nutbag in the bathroom."

"That make him a good guy?" Cheo said.

"I dunno. Hard to tell, ain't it?"

"Yeah. We should have a 'run' signal."

Pete nodded. "Curve ball," he said, holding down two fingers. "That's the sign. Curve ball we run, fastball we stay."

"Hssst!" It was him, it was Dzekas, he was back, but the change in his appearance was startling. He had a pair of shades perched high on his forehead, and the bathrobe was gone. In its place was a black polo shirt that proclaimed how much the wearer hearted New York. "Come on, youse two, let's go," he said.

Cheo and Pete, both glad to get out of the black tunnel, clambered up to join him on the platform. "They leave?" Cheo asked Dzekas. "What happened to your bathrobe?"

"Trashed it," Dzekas said, grinning. "They're selling these up to the newsstand. Fetching, don't you think?"

"Cool," Cheo said. They headed for the stairs to get out.

"Listen," Dzekas said. "They didn't see me before. Not really. All they seen was some old wino. Another lost soul, that's all. And they won't see me in this neither, they'll just see another dipshit tourist. People mostly see what they wanna see. Only God sees who you really are. And yeah, they're gone, I think, but you can't be sure. I stuck that phone inside some lady's baby carriage, so most of them are gonna be following her back up to The Bronx, but if it was me, I'd leave someone behind to watch. See if we come out after they go."

Pete stopped. "Then shouldn't we wait?"

"Nah. See, them Greeks and those two cops, they seem be working together but don't none of them trust each other. And there's one Black guy with them, I don't know who he is but if I was him I wouldn't trust a one of them. So even if it would be smart for one of them to stay behind and watch, none of them wants to do it for fear of being cut out of whatever kind of deal they made with each other. You guys hungry? I'm starving."

"We don't got money for breakfast," Cheo told him.

"Money ain't the problem," Dzekas told him. "Don't worry, I got you."

"You ain't a bum?" Pete asked him.

"Didn't say that," Dzekas said. "But I'm buying breakfast."

He got them a table in the window of a small coffee shop. His eyes scanned the crowds going by on Lexington Avenue.

"So you saw Pelios," Cheo said. "You talked to him after he got out."

Dzekas nodded. "I did him a solid, I guess. Got him out of a tough spot."

"So how come you're not with them any more?" Pete said. "Tasya and them guys."

"I made it too hard for God to get my attention," Dzekas said.

"What?" Cheo said.

Dzekas looked at Cheo. "I know you ain't a believer," he said. "Not yet. That's all right, you're a smart kid, you'll catch on. But the fact is, God was giving me signs. You know, messages. He was trying to make me see that the way I was living was not what he wanted for me, but I didn't want to hear him. I had it too good, I thought, I had money, I had cars, I had women, I had everything. So what if I hadda hack off a couple toes here and there? So I closed up my ears and I pretended I didn't hear nothing. I don't think God was too happy when I done that. Same thing happen to Jonah, you know. God sent him to Nineveh, Jonah didn't wanna go, look what happened to him, dude got swallowed down by a whale. You don't mess with the man, you hear what I'm saying?"

Pete and Cheo exchanged a look. "You think that really happened?"

"I ain't sure," Dzekas said. "The whale part is tough to buy, I know, but one thing is for certain, God kicked Jonah's bony ass all the way to Nineveh whether he wanted to go there or not."

"You didn't get swallowed by a whale."

"No, no I didn't. I pushed my luck too far, though, I promise you that, and I got my butt kicked for it."

"What do you mean?" Pete said.

"Came a day, I knew I had to choose. Either I was to listen to what the good lord was trying to tell me, or I was to keep on the way I was, and pay the price. Well, I chose wrong, I kept on. And I'm paying the price."

"Kept on what?" Pete said.

Dzekas sighed. "We owned the baggage handlers out to the airports," he said. "If you wanted to get something into the country without anybody asking no questions about it, you came to us, we got it in for you. For a percentage, you understand."

"Drugs," Cheo said.

Dzekas shrugged. "Whatever. Didn't matter to us. You got it on the plane, we got it off. All the baggage handlers and cargo guys were on the payroll. You couldn't get a job out there unless you was with us. So one day, one of the guys on the baggage crew dies. Which happens. In this particular case, his wife caught him fooling around, he had the poor judgement to be married to a Greek woman and she stuck him with a kitchen knife and that were the end of him. So now we got an open slot. We're wondering who we could use, you know, because it has to be someone we can trust. We finally settle on this one guy, he's a kid from the neighborhood. He's not a bad kid, smokes a little weed now and then but who don't, you know, but he ain't no doper or nothing like that. His mother used to be a party girl back in the day, a lot of us knew her pretty well, you know what I'm saying. We used to joke about it, 'hey, he's got your nose, he's got to be your kid,' stuff like that. So we put him on.

"Everything works out good.

"Then it turns out, he's got a girlfriend up in Boston, he flies up there once a month to visit her. No biggie, right? But check it out, this chick is a lawyer. Not only is she a lawyer, all right, but she's an assistant D.A. With the Commonwealth of Massachusetts." He sighed. "Probably didn't mean nothing. Probably was just what he said it was, they met, they fell in love, blah blah blah. And it seemed to me that she was too young, I couldn't see the them setting her up to run some kinda sting on us. But in this game you don't take no chances."

He sighed again. "We had him in the basement of this house in Corona. He's crying, right, swearing on his mother's life that it ain't nothing, he would never roll over on us. It was terrible. I mean, I know this kid since he's a baby." He looked at Cheo and Pete. "That was my chance. And I blew it. We done what we always done, even though I knew it was wrong."

"You killed him?"

"We did. And I hadda pay the price. The good lord finally got my attention."

"What are you talking about?" Cheo said.

"I got sick," Dzekas told him. "I come down bad sick a few weeks later. Funny, how everybody runs for cover when you get sick. Time I got done with the doctors, I looked like this." He held his hands out, palms up. "No hair, down about a hundred pounds, pains in my gut like you wouldn't believe. Doctors said to go home and put my affairs in order. Whatever that means. Anyway, I never went back to the old crowd. Didn't see the point. I'd started thinking, what happens when I die? I didn't have nobody, you know what I mean? Didn't have no one to leave it all with, so what the hell good was it? What good was anything? But I'm walking down the street one day, feeling low, and I hear singing. It was the Bedford Street Tabernacle. So I go in, and the Reverend Davis shows me the truth of it all. God was just giving me one last chance to atone for what I been." He fished a small bottle out of his pocket and took a few dark green capsules out of it. Grimacing, he popped them into his mouth and swallowed.

"What's that?" Pete said.

Dzekas stowed the bottle. "Necessary evil," he said. "But they take fifteen, twenty minutes to kick in, so whattaya say we stick here for a little while?" He reached into another pocket and fished out a wad of cash, peeled off a twenty and handed it to Pete. "Do me a favor, okay kid? Get me a large tea with milk, no sugar. Some toast, no butter. And whatever you guys want."

Pete glanced at Cheo. Cheo shrugged, held down one finger. Pete headed for the counter. "I thought you was broke," Cheo said. "On account of the pan-handling."

"That's what you was supposed to think," Dzekas told him. "Nobody wants to know you when you ain't got none, so they don't look at you good. If the police was to ask them people back on the train what they seen, whattaya suppose they'd say?"

Cheo nodded. "Crazy old homeless guy with no shirt."

"Exactly. And if they walked right by this window and looked in at me, not a one of them would reckanize me."

"I knew there was something about you. Knew it when you was looking over at us, back at the subway station."

"You're smarter'n you look, you know that? And now you know what I am but you figure to keep me talking and you might find out more. I already told you I used to be one of them."

"One of the Greeks," Cheo said, nodding. "But then God smacked you in the head."

Dzekas nodded ruefully.

"I still don't get it," Cheo said. "If you ain't with them any more, why are you here?"

"See, you're still too young, you don't understand. You don't know nothing about money, and so far you prolly ain't done nothing worth repenting of. Shit, I bet you ain't even learned how to play spank the monkey yet."

Cheo swallowed. "I gotta repent that?"

Dzekas snorted. "You can't tell me that God gives one wet fart about a thing like that. Now the Reverend Davis, he'll tell you different, but you can't believe everything these religious ding-dongs tell you, most of 'em ain't seen enough badness to know what's evil and what ain't, but I seen some evil in my time, and I tell you what, little brother, the day's coming when you will, too. When it does, you better be smarter than me. Don't wait until it's too late."

"How can it be too late?" Cheo asked him. "You ain't dead yet."

"No, not quite," Dzekas said. "The Reverend Davis says God loves me, though my sins be as scarlet, which by God they are. But that's coming from a man that ain't stole as much as a pack of cigarettes in his whole life, believe that or not. So I got to figure my chances are pretty slim. My best shot..." He leaned both forearms on the table and stared intently at Cheo. "I mean, I could be way off here, but my best shot, I figure, is if I get lucky and go on a day when they're busy as hell." He lowered his voice, went on in a conspiratorial tone. "You know, on a day when there's an airline crash, or one of them big cruise ships goes down, or a giant earthquake. Something like that. And St. Peter be there with his keys, right, he's gonna be thinking, 'God, I am gonna be stuck out here all frickin' day,' and when he gets to me, okay, the book will tell him what I done. The good and the bad. If I'm lucky he won't read the whole bad page, the size of the type oughta tell the story anyhow, but there on the good side it'll say how in the end I repented, and how I built the Reverend Davis a new Tabernacle. I figure him and the Reverend Davis gotta be pretty tight."

"That's why you want Pelios's money," Cheo said. "I thought money was the root of all evil."

"Yeah, well, so did I," Dzekas told him. "Even though, I have to say, it's a powerful convenience. Long as I got my ATM card, for example, I can sleep anywhere I want. But the Reverend Davis says it ain't the thing of itself that's evil, it's the wanting of it so bad that you'd be willing to do most anything to lay your hands on it. Like the Greeks, the ones that's looking for you."

Pete came back with three paper cups and a small bag on a plastic tray. He put the tray down and piled Dzekas' change in front of him, then put one of the cups next to it.

"Thank you, son." Dzekas stared at the other two cups hungrily. "That coffee you got there?"

Pete shook his head. "Hot chocolates."

"Oh," Dzekas said, disappointed. "I hate tea. God, what I would give for a nice cup a coffee."

"You want me to change this?" Pete said, reaching for the cup.

"No, no," Dzekas told him. "I can't have coffee no more, tea is as close as I can get to it, which is a piss-poor substitute, you ask me."

"How about a donut?" Pete said, opening the bag. "This toast don't look too swingin'."

"Nope, can't have no donuts neither. You two go ahead."

"So what's a tabernacle, anyhow?" Cheo asked him. "How much you figure it's gonna cost you?"

"Oh, it ain't nothing but a big room," Dzekas said. "With enough space for wooden pews. And why they want them is beyond me, you got to sit there all morning long listening, least you ought for crissake to have a comfortable chair to do it in. But anyhow, they got the property already, I figure they could put up a decent enough building for about a deuce. Two hundred thou. Now, I got about a hundred, okay, which I saved outa my own ill-gotten gains, but I don't know how much of that is gonna be left. Seventy-five, eighty, maybe. So I figure that leaves me a buck and a quarter short, give or take."

"So, what?" Cheo said. "You just gonna take all your money and put it in a bag and give it to the Reverend and he builds the tabernacle? By himself?"

"No," Dzekas said, "hell, no. The Reverend Davis don't know one end of a hammer from the other. He's what you might call a spiritual creature, anyhow, when it comes to practical shit, he ain't got the sense God gave a goose. But there's a couple good hard men in his congregation, there, I'm thinking they could get her built."

"You think Pelios left enough money behind to get it done?"

Dzekas nodded. Cheo figured his green pills must be doing their work, because the man's face seemed to be unclenching. "Wouldn't take but a smidge, anyhow," Dzekas said. He pushed a tiny crumb across the table. "Like that right there next to your donut. And if I'm wrong, which I ain't, I won't take nothing, I'll just give up the seventy-five and hope for the best, you boys can go ahead and keep whatever we find. Now I know you fellas got no reason to trust me, but I'm giving you my word."

"Well you did get us away from that guy in the subway," Pete said.

"That don't hardly count," Dzekas said. "Anybody woulda done that. Now there's a guy going straight to hell."

"For, um..."

"Being gay? Or whatever the hell he is? Nah. Nobody with any sense really gives a shit about that. No, it's because he didn't give you shelter when he coulda. For treating you like he done. He'll burn for that, you mark my words. Now listen to me, here. I know where you guys are going, everybody knew which graveyard Gaitanis went to when he wanted to visit his poor dead mother or to stash some dough, okay, that wasn't no secret. There's gonna be people waiting, you catch my drift. Youse two got some kind of a plan?"

Cheo and Pete looked at each other, then at Dzekas. "What kinda plan?" Pete said.

"Well, now, believe it or not, I ain't much for tactics," Dzekas said. "Just go straight after it, that's my opinion. Like a bulldozer. Except I don't think it would be the proper approach here, not for you two guys. To begin with, I was you, I'd wait until after dark."

"After dark?" Pete sounded horrified.

"After dark," Dzekas replied, nodding his head. "That way you got a chance. Slip on in there like a coupla burglars, grab what you come for and slip back on out."

"I got a question," Cheo said. "Exactly what is it that we're supposed to be looking for? I don't know how much me and Pete can carry."

Dzekas scratched his chin. "Wondered about that myself. I don't see it like most of them. They all think, all's they need is the number of the mausoleum, okay, then they'll go bust on in there and find stacks of hundreds, boxes of jewelries, gold bars and whatnot." He shook his head. "Gaitanis, he was too smart for that. Way too smart. Everybody knows he didn't like banks, okay, but they don't know that it wasn't nothing to do with the banks theirselves, if you catch my drift. What he didn't like was the idea that the powers that be, or even his wife's lawyers, you know what I'm saying, could go looking to see what he had in his accounts. That's all it was. To Gaitanis' way of thinking, what he had stashed away wasn't nobody's business but his own. You catch my meaning?"

"No," Cheo said.

Dzekas nodded. "See, no offense, kiddo, but like I said, you don't know nothing about money. Or women, neither. Money is like battery acid, you can use it but it'll burn you, it'll eat a hole in your pocket, you got to treat it with respect. What you're gonna do when you get rich, okay, you're gonna walk into a bank and you're gonna rent a safety deposit box. That's like your own private safe. See, everything you put in there is between you and the good lord. Your girlfriend ain't gonna know you got it, Uncle Sam ain't gonna know, so neither of them can pester you to give them some. And you're gonna fill up that box, you hear me, and you're gonna walk outa that bank with the key in your pocket, and you're gonna stash that key someplace safe. Like, under the floormat of your car, maybe. Now Gaitanis, he had too much money for one box, he had too much money for a dozen boxes, so he prolly thought of something else, but it'll be the same kind of situation. So while the rest of them are looking for diamonds and gold, you gotta be thinking, you gotta be looking at everything, okay, because the answer is something a smart man would think of. Not a dope like me. Something he could leave right out in plain sight, like right on his desk, and alla his thieving relatives would walk right on past without looking at it twice."

"Like a stamp collection," Pete said.

"You see?" Dzekas said. "Smart guy."

"Or a key ring," Cheo said.

"You got it. You got it. But your first problem is getting in without getting caught. I'd wait until it's nice and dark, which means you're gonna have to hang around for a while." He squinted out the window at the sun. "Long while. And don't wait down by the graveyard, neither, nothing good can come from that. Listen, you don't mind me asking, did Pelios give you any idea what you was up against?"

"No," Cheo said. "Just said the eyes would tell us where to look."

Dzekas looked thoughtful. "You don't say. The eyes. Hunh. You two got any money for lunch?"

"No," Cheo said.

Dzekas reached into a pocket. "Seein' how we're partners now..." He glanced up, caught the look Cheo and Pete gave each other. "Oh, stop worrying. It's just a limited partnership, I told you guys that. So here's my buy-in, for now." He handed each of them a twenty.

"We'll pay you back," Pete told him.

Dzekas got a funny look on his face. "No need," he said.

"Why not?" Pete said.

"'As you done the least of my brothers, you done it to me.' Something like that. I heard the Reverend Davis read it right out of the scripture. Heard it with my own two ears."

"What's it mean?" Cheo said.

"Well, you know what, I ain't totally sure, but I'm guessing it means you got to help out the short guys because they never catch a break. Which, no offense, would be youse two. So now you ain't quite as short as you was. Might give St. Pete one more little thing to read offa the right-hand page, you know what I'm sayin. Now here's the deal; I'm gonna leave youse two on your own, you just keep your heads down 'till it's good and dark out. I'm gonna go see if I can even up the odds a little bit."

"What do you mean?"

"Don't worry," Dzekas said, and he winked. "Since I'm after building a tabernacle, here, I figure I'm a soldier working the Lord's vineyard, and if a coupla grapes get stomped on here and there, you know what I mean, that's just the cost of doing business, ain't it?" He stood up. "Watch for me."

"Can I ask you one thing?" Cheo said. "Why didn't you just ask Pelios for the money when you saw him?"

"I did," he said. "Promised him I'd stay on the sidelines, wouldn't give Tasya or Vasilios a heads-up about where he was or what he was doin'. But now Pelios is among the missing, and here I stand, chasing it just like they are."

"Except without a little silver knife," Cheo told him.

"There's that," Dzekas said. "You two be careful, now. Watch your butts. I'll see you later on."

CHAPTER 9

"Do you believe in ghosts?

Cheo noted the carefully modulated tone of his friend's voice. He's being careful, Cheo thought. Trying to sound normal. He doesn't wanna sound like he's feeling it. Pete, who shook off without comment the beatings a catcher routinely took from errant pitches, foul balls and wild backswings, who could hit a ball farther than anyone else Cheo knew, who was built like a brick with feet and was just about as hard, Pete, his friend, was shaken by the idea of sneaking into a graveyard after dark. "Never seen one," Cheo said. "You?"

"On Hart Island," Pete said. "Just across the bay from where I live. That's where they have Potter's Field."

"What's potter's field?" Cheo said.

"It's where the city buries people that nobody knows who they are. Like homeless guys and stuff. They been doing it ever since we chased the Indians away. There's got to be like a zillion dead guys out there."

"So? You ever see any of 'em?"

"Sometimes you can see lights moving around over there at night," Pete said. "My mom says they're lost souls trying to find a way to get off the island."

Your mom has blue hair, Cheo thought, but he didn't say it. "How does she know they're not just lights from the cars up on Pelham Parkway or whatever? Does she really believe in ghosts?"

Pete laughed but it didn't sound like he really thought anything was funny. "Who knows what she believes," he said. "But she talks about them like they're real." They walked on in silence for about half a block. "Then again," Pete said, "she talks that way about fairies, too. And unicorns, and UFOs, and Harry Potter."

Cheo, who got lost in Harry Potter every time one of the movies played on cable, found himself liking Pete's mother a little more, blue hair or not. "Maybe she's just into Harry Potter," he said. "That don't have to mean she thinks it's real."

"Did you read the books?"

Cheo didn't answer right away. If word got out at school, there would be repercussions. People would start calling him 'Harry Pothead,' and who needed that? But he trusted Pete would keep his mouth shut so he risked it. "Yeah," he finally said. "You?"

"No," Pete said. "I seen the movies. But I never believed in it."

"I know what you mean."

"If I thought I seen a ghost," Pete said, "I think I would probably crap in my pants."

"If you think you see a ghost, okay," Cheo said, "what you should do is look for the scam. 'Cause it ain't a ghost, it's just somebody trying to con you."

"For real," Pete said, his face somber. "You ain't afraid of ghosts?"

"Yo, Pete, you don't need no made-up shit to be scared of. There's already plenty of for real things to worry about."

"Like what?"

"Bears," Cheo said. "I seen this show on the nature channel where they had polar bears at a zoo and this one kid messed around and climbed over the fence, right, and the polar bear killed him. And then he ate him."

Pete shivered. "That's terrible," he said. "But there ain't no polar bears in The Bronx."

"Maybe not," Cheo said. "But they got tigers at The Bronx zoo. Same thing."

"You dope, how is a tiger the same thing as a bear?"

"They both kill you and eat you."

Pete laughed. "Why would you care? If you're already dead, what difference does it make if they eat you or not?"

"First of all," Cheo said, "I don't want anything killing me, and second of all, I don't want anything eating me, either."

"I think the odds are pretty good nothing's gonna eat either one of us this trip," Pete said.

"Maybe not," Cheo said.

"So okay," Pete said. "You ain't afraid of ghosts, but your list has bears and tigers on it. What else?"

"My mother," Cheo said, "who is gonna kill me when we get back."

"Probably. What else?"

"Coach, who is never gonna let me throw my curveball again. Besides, what about you?"

"What about me?"

"What's on your list? Ghosts, and what else?"

"Uncle Teddy," Pete said.

"Who's he?"

"He's not my uncle, he's just this guy. Always looks, like, sweaty. They say he'll give you ten bucks if you go over his house. And the kids that go, they always look sweaty too, when they come back."

"Okay," Cheo said. "You don't gotta draw me a map. What else?"

"Dzekas," Pete answered, "who is crazy, and probably does believe in ghosts. And that lady who chased us in the subway station. And that nut case that was hanging around in the subway bathroom. They would all kill us, but at least they wouldn't eat us."

"Don't bet on it," Cheo said. "That Greek lady might eat you if she thought of it. Mmm, Pete, sliced thin, on a roll, with mustard."

"Chunks of Cheo," Pete said, "on a stick, with BBQ sauce."

"Serious, Pete, are we gonna walk all the way to Queens? I don't wanna go back on the subway, they're gonna be looking for us down there."

"Don't worry, there's plenty of ways to get where you're going on the train, we just gotta walk until we get to a different line. Like the L, maybe, on 14th Street."

"You really know a lot about the trains."

"My mom says every New York kid should know how to get around. It ain't no big thing. Question is what are we gonna do when we get there?"

"Wait until dark, like Dzekas said. And then if we can get in without getting caught, we do it. Otherwise, screw it, we go home. Deal?"

"Deal. But if we see any ghosts, I say we take off."

Times Square is a coral reef, a crazy dance of color, motion, and money, sharks, lionfish, barracuda, yellow jacks and a thousand more, the predators circling while the baitfish mass together in clouds, thinking they might be safer if they stick together. Morays lurk in the darker corners, waiting for passers-by who are distracted by the flashing lights. No one wants to get eaten but everybody knows it happens every day so they keep moving, trying to avoid the more obvious hazards. Cheo had never been to Times Square before, and considering himself neither a prey animal nor a predator, he had no intention of ever going back. He and Pete slithered through the crowds of adults, Cheo scowling, doing his best to watch everyone at once. He wanted to ask Pete why they had come this way but it was too noisy and besides, Cheo knew that there is generally no good answer to why. Times Square was simply where they were and they just needed to find a way to get through it. They paused at an intersection to wait for a flood of yellow cabs to pass. On the opposite corner three hustlers played three-card monte, which is not a game at all but is, instead, a reliable way to separate a gullible person from his money. The dealer was in the midst of sliding three beat-up cards around face down on the bottom of a cardboard box. The dumber tourists paused to watch while the smarter ones slid out around and passed on by. The dealer glanced up, looked across at Cheo and Pete and then he and his compatriots were gone, cardboard box, cards and all, all three guys like smoke in the breeze, vanishing in four different directions. It took Cheo and Pete a few seconds to work that one out and by that time it was too late, a cop in a blue uniform had them both, one in each of his big meaty paws.

"Gentlemen," he said. "Who might you be? And what are you doing all on your own in a place like this?"

The light changed and suddenly the cop and the two kids were the obstacle and the baitfish circled them warily. The cop had a partner who had stopped about ten feet away and was speaking into a radio. "We ain't done nothing," Pete told the first one. "We was just walking."

"Well, then, you got nothing to worry about, do you?"

Cheo and Pete both knew what an outright lie that was but neither of them laughed. The cop looked over his shoulder at his partner. "What's the word?"

"Hold 'em," his partner said. "Glass says it sounds like them."

"Oh, crap," Cheo said. The cop holding him broke into a big grin.

"Oh, yeah," he said. "You can run but you can't hide. What did you two desperadoes do to attract the attention of a man like Detective Glass?"

"You know him?" Cheo said.

"I know of him. Quit worrying, he just wants to ask you a couple of questions."

"I bet," Pete said.

Glass and Alcantare arrived moments later in separate cabs, maybe thirty seconds apart. Glass was first. He wore a wrinkled brown suit and he looked pissed. He and Cheo scowled at each other. "What the hell did you do with that cell phone I gave you?" he said.

"What the hell were you thinking when you bought that suit?" Cheo asked him. The two uniformed policemen both laughed, which did not seem to improve Glass's mood. Alcantare got out of his cab right about then, and seeing the two uniforms smiling, he smiled back, even when he noticed the expression on his partner's face.

"Hey, great," he said. "You got 'em." He rubbed his palms together.

The two uniformed policemen did not immediately recognize him as a policeman and they both turned to face him, their eyes going cold. It was a subtle change but Cheo could feel the tension in the hand that gripped his shoulder.

"It's all right," Glass said. He didn't look all that happy to see his partner. "He's one of ours." He turned back to Cheo. "What?" he said. "You wanna tell me how to dress now?"

"What?" Cheo said. "You really wanna go around looking like you get your clothes at the Starvation Army?"

"Sal-vation, you nimrod," Pete said.

"Shut the hell up, both of you," Glass said.

"All right, all right, all right," Alcantare said, sliding up and assuming custody of Cheo and Pete. "Lighten up," he told Glass. "They're just kids." He squeezed Cheo's shoulder. "And you don't have to be such a hard-on. The guy was worried about you."

"Sure he was," Cheo said.

"Somebody stole the phone," Pete said, and he leaned forward to wink at Cheo. It wasn't an entire wink, more of a twitch of one eye but Pete was Cheo's catcher and they knew each other well. It was, Cheo knew, Pete's way of telling to relax. Quit worrying. I got this.

"Someone stole it," Glass said flatly, skeptical.

Pete nodded. "On the subway."

Glass shook his head. "That's what you get for riding the goddam trains," he said. "Down in a hole in the ground with the animals."

"All right," Alcantare said again. He looked at the two uniformed policemen. "Thanks, guys. We'll take it from here. We're gonna find a nice quiet place where we can talk."

The two uniforms, particularly the one that had been holding Cheo and Pete, looked unsure, like they weren't quite ready to turn around and walk away. "Don't worry," Alcantare told him. "It's all good."

"Let's go," Glass growled, and he headed for a side street, out of the square. The crowds avoided him, baitfish avoiding him like he was one of the more ill-tempered predators, and Alcantare followed, still holding on to Cheo and Pete. Cheo turned to glare at the two uniforms. You see? he thought as he stared at them. You see what you did? The uniformed cops watched, looking somewhat ill at ease.

The place Glass picked out was a dive, a dark and smelly Indian restaurant halfway down a shaded block. Glass got them all seated at a round table just inside the doorway. There was a single waiter in the joint and when he approached, Glass turned on him, holding his police I.D. up in the man's face. "Take a walk, shithead," he snarled. "We're gonna use this table for ten minutes and we don't wanna hear from you."

The man's face flushed with anger but he backed away after staring at Glass's I.D. for a second or two.

"Why you gotta be so hostile?" Alcantare asked him, his voice lowered. "You coulda had him bring us something to drink. Let the poor sucker make a buck."

"Later," Glass said. "Take care of business first."

Alcantare shook his head. "Whatever." He looked at Cheo. "You guys were supposed to call us," he said. "You were gonna call us if anything happened. How are we supposed to keep an eye on you if you bail out on us?"

"You two think you're funny," Glass snarled. He grabbed the nearest chair and plopped himself down in it, but then immediately moved to one further into the room, away from the weak glow coming through the grimy front window. "You little bastards won't be laughing when we stick your little asses in a holding cell downtown in the Tombs. The animals we keep in there will eat the both of you for lunch. I bet you won't find that so goddam amusing."

Alcantare held up a hand and Glass went silent. "Detective Glass is just upset," he said, leaning forward across the table to stare at Cheo and Pete. "You guys had us worried, taking off like that."

"What were we supposed to tell you?" Cheo said. "'Oh, Officer, Pelios showed up at our game.' So what? You guys were both there, I seen you both. You seen the same things we did."

"What did he say to you?" Glass said.

"He told Cheo that he had a great curve ball," Pete said. "He told me I blew it by standing up to catch it. Said I gotta sell it better so the ump will call it a strike. And he told us not to worry about Coach getting all honked off at us for using it in a game."

Glass threw his hands up. "Oh, for crissake..."

Alcantare cut in. "No, no, that's all right," he said, waving at Glass. The gesture looked, to Cheo, like the same one Pete used to tell Cheo to keep his pitches down. "The kid's right, Cheo does have a nice curve. And he's right, we were there, we saw what happened. But come on, guys, work with me here. You know what we're talking about. Give me something. Give me something to work with so that Detective Glass over here doesn't blow a gasket, because you don't want that." He leaned in closer and lowered his voice. "You might think he's bluffing, but he's not. He could do it, and worse. Glass is capable of some awful things, believe me. You don't wanna go there. I don't wanna go there. Okay? So let's keep this as civilized as we possibly can. Just tell me what Pelios said to you guys. Especially the parts that don't pertain to baseball." He nodded, like they'd already agreed. "We're the police. Do you understand what that means? That means we're the good guys. We work for you, and for your moms, and for all the other good guys. Okay? Okay?"

Pete turned to look at Cheo and his eye twitched again. "All right," Pete said. "He won't tell you, but I will." He held two fingers under the table, down where only Cheo could see them.

It was the 'run' sign.

Glass leaned in and put an elbow on the table. Alcantare seemed like he was frozen in place. Cheo breathed deeply, preparing himself. "He told us that everybody thinks that the money is buried in the cemetery," Pete said.

"Cavalry," Alcantare breathed.

"Cal-vary," Pete corrected him.

"You see?" Glass muttered. "Even the damn kids are smarter than you."

"Shut up," Alcantare snapped. He looked at Pete. "Go on."

Pete held down five fingers. "There's no money there. But there is a map."

Four fingers.

"It's in a pink envelope."

Three fingers.

"It's buried next to a headstone with a Russian name on it."

Two fingers.

"Okay, good," Alcantare said. "Now we're getting somewhere. What's the name?"

One finger.

"Hugh," Pete whispered.

Glass and Alcantare were both completely still. Pete folded his last finger into his fist and shook the fist once. "Hugh Bichapeckerov," he said.

Glass blew up. "Son of a...." Alcantare turned to hold his partner back and at that instant Pete and Cheo both exploded out of their chairs and took off.

Outside on the street it looked like they had nowhere to go. The lights and sounds of Times Square were at least a half a block away and there was no way Cheo and Pete could get there in the seconds they probably had before before Glass and Alcantare came out the door after them. There was a van parked in the street, though, painted in the blue and white colors of Con Edison. It had a flashing yellow light on top.

They made it underneath the van with no time to spare.

The door to the restaurant banged open. The boys couldn't see the two cops but they could hear them perfectly well, mostly Glass's voice cursing and yelling at Alcantare.

"Never mind that!" Alcantare finally yelled back. "You wanna blame it all on me? Fine! But if you hadn't been such an asshole, maybe they wouldn't have taken off! Besides, they can't get far. You go that way, I'm going up to the square, we'll meet back here in ten. Right here."

Cheo and Pete looked at each other. Pete held up two fingers, but it was more of a question. Do we run? Cheo shook his head, held up one finger instead. He leaned over and whispered into Pete's ear. "They're at both ends of the block, they'll see us coming from a mile away."

Pete looked worried. "They know where we're going. The cemetery."

"So what," Cheo said. "They still gotta catch us. What's Calvary mean, anyhow?"

"I don't know," Pete said. "It's a church word. How long do we wait here?"

"They said they was coming back in ten," Cheo said. "Let's see what they do after they don't find us and they meet back here."

Alcantare was back first, he came walking back from Time's Square about ten minutes later, he was accompanied by the uniformed policeman who had grabbed Cheo and Pete. The boys laid quiet and still on the dirty street as the two cops approached. "Whaddaya mean they got away?" Cheo recognized the cop's voice. "You have got to be joking. How did the two of you let a couple a kids just walk away from you?"

"They didn't walk," Alcantare's voice said sourly. "Anyway, you hadda be there. Maybe Glass caught 'em."

"Listen." The cop's voice dropped low. "You're Glass's partner. What happened to him? My uncle told me Glass was one of the best cops he ever worked with. They still tell stories about him down at Midtown South. He looks like he's gone to seed. You think it's the booze?"

"Aaaagh." Alcantare sounded disgusted. His foot kicked a bottle cap that was lying on the sidewalk and it flew under the van, missing Pete's head by inches before it rattled out into the middle of 43rd Street. "It was the divorce," he said. "The booze didn't come until later."

"Lotta guys get divorced," the cop said, leaving his accusation unvoiced.

Alcantare sighed. "Yeah, no kidding. But his ex-wife was a lawyer, man, she cleaned him out. She took everything but his skivvies. He ain't been the same since. Aw crap, here he comes. He didn't get 'em neither. Do me a favor, just hang out here for a minute or two, when he gets here tell him I went back up to the square to check it out one more time."

Alcantare's feet took off, not running but not wasting any time, either. The uniformed cop's shiny black shoes took two steps over to wait by the curb, and a moment later Glass's scuffed brogans walked up. "Where'd he go."

"Said he wanted to check the square out again."

"Yeah, okay," Glass said. "I'll tell you what he wants. He wants me to wear myself out yelling at you so he don't have to listen to it."

"Maybe so. Listen, do you remember a guy named Taciak? From your days back at Midtown South."

"Who could forget a name like that?" Glass said. "Yeah, I remember him. Good cop. Taught me a lot."

"My uncle," the cop said.

"No kidding! How the hell is he?"

"Ah, well, he passed. Retirement didn't agree with him, I guess. But I still remember the stories he told about you. He said you were one of the best. Said you'd wind up in the commissioner's office before you were through."

"Ain't gonna happen," Glass said. "Sorry to hear about your uncle, though. He eat his gun?"

The cop didn't answer the question. "What happened, if you don't mind me asking. What went wrong?"

Glass's feet walked around to the front of the van and turned towards Times Square. His heels faced Cheo and Pete, just feet away under the van, which creaked when Glass leaned his weight on it. "She divorced him, didn't she? Mrs. Taciak."

"How'd you know?"

"It's the job," Glass said. "Being a cop. It sucks the life out of you. If you're a dirtbag it don't matter much, you got nothing in you to begin with but if you're a decent guy, it rots your soul. Time you get your thirty years in and you're ready to quit, you got nothing left. You're like one of those old trees, people walking by, they look at you and think you're fine but your insides are all rotted away, a storm blows through and it'll knock you right over. Then they all say, 'ooh, look at that, he was standing there all dead in the middle, ain't that a shame,' and then they walk right on by."

"Being a policeman is just a job," the other cop said. "I agree it can be stressful, but..."

"Stressful?" It was beginning to sound like Alcantare was going to get his wish, but then Glass seemed to pull it together again. "Listen, kid. Let me ask you something. How many times you carry a baby out of some apartment house, dead because it's mother got sick of it crying and locked it in a closet and left it there? How many females you scrape up off the street because her boyfriend got sick of her shit and pitched her off the balcony? Hmm? How many times you bust your ass to make a case on some drug dealer and then watch him walk past you smiling with them gold teeth and go right on back to work? Shit. And then you go home and your wife wants to know how your day went. And you can't tell her because you're afraid of what might come out of your mouth if you open it? How my day went? Are you kidding me? But you're not *communicating*. You don't *love* her like you used to. And then the day comes when the streets are real and your wife, your kids and your house are not that real any more, they're more like a daydream. That's when you wake up and you know it's too late. You're lost. I tell you what, kid. I try to do one decent thing every day, you hear me? And you seem like a good guy, so today's gonna be your lucky day: quit.

Forget about bein' a cop. Quit while you still got a soul. Walk away. Go on back to school, drive a bus, go buy a deli, sell newspapers, anything you can think of is better than this. Get out while you still can."

"Can I ask you one question?" the cop said.

"One more," Glass told him.

"What you want with them two kids?"

The van creaked again as Glass pushed himself away from it. "My wife? The one I couldn't *communicate* with? She got the house and the kids. She got most of my paycheck and half of my pension. I'm trapped in a burning house, okay? There's only one window and those two damned kids are holding it shut. Here comes Alcantare, God, he musta went somewhere so he could do a quick number, he gets any higher he's gonna hafta call LaGuardia and file a flight plan. I mean it, kid. Get out. Go back to school or something."

Alcantare's gray sneakers showed up a moment later. "Couldn't find 'em."

"Don't matter, I guess," Glass said. "We know where they're going. Calvary cemetery. Come on." His beat-up shoes took a couple of steps toward Times Square.

"Still gotta catch 'em," Alcantare said.

Glass stopped, and he turned around once more. "Hey, kid. Your uncle. Old man Taciak. He eat his gun? He shoot himself?"

For a moment there was no answer.

"Yeah," the guy finally said. "Yeah, he did."

"Thought so," Glass said. "Because he was a good man. A sensitive soul. The job got to him. Remember what I told you. Don't wait until it's too late."

"What are you guys talking about?" Alcantare said.

"Nothing you gotta worry about," Glass said. "Come on, let's go."

Glass's brogans and Alcantare's running shoes disappeared in the direction of Times Square.

A few minutes later, two women standing in front of a theatre across the street watched without comment as Cheo and Pete slid out from under the van. The boys took off west on 43rd, not in a panic, not exactly, but without any wasted motion. They kept it up for some time, putting some space between themselves and Glass, Alcantare, and the two uniformed patrolmen. They didn't stop to rest until they got over to Manhattan's west side. They wound up across the street from what looked like a red brick parking garage, except that there was a horse-drawn carriage parked out in front, a white horse with blinders on standing silent and still in the harness, staring down at the road. From the smell coming out through the open doors, there had to be more horses inside. The horse out front gave no sign that he was either dead or alive. "Not as crowded over here," Pete said.

"That's like saying, 'hey, there ain't as many fleas down on this end of the dog,'" Cheo said.

"Sheesh," Pete said. "That's where they keep the horses? Don't they belong in a pasture somewhere? What a stink."

"I dunno. These are city horses," Cheo said. "This is all they get. It ain't their fault that their garage smells bad."

"Smells better than that cop," Pete said.

"Which one?"

"The one in the brown suit, who said that everything in his life was our fault."

"Glass."

"Yeah," Pete said. "What kinda cop smells like beer this early on a Sunday? And how about, like, taking a shower? And having a shave? You think that might make a difference for him?"

"Maybe he's having a bad weekend," Cheo said.

"Sounds more like a bad year, you ask me. Him and his pothead partner." Pete was getting hot.

"He wants the money," Cheo said. "Pelios said this was gonna happen. He said…" The lights of realization dawned in Cheo's eyes. "That prick."

"Who?"

"Pelios! He set us up. Check it out. Everybody who was trying to get that money was chasing after Pelios, right, and then at the ball game, right in front of everybody, he gives us this stupid key, and then he takes off. Now they all think he's dead and they can't chase after him any more. What's that leave them?"

"You and me," Pete said.

"Yeah. You and me."

"I don't know if they all saw him leave the key…"

"Don't matter," Cheo said. "We were the last guys he talked to before he ran, so now everybody thinks we know something. You remember? That was the first thing Glass and Alcantare wanted to know. 'What'd he say, what'd he tell you.' I wonder if this key even works. I wonder if it even opens anything."

"So all we gotta do is stay away from Glass and Alcantare, right, plus Tasya Gaitanis and her guys, and whoever else might be sneaking up on us, find a way into Calvary without any of them seeing us, steal the money and get home alive. That's it."

"Yeah," Cheo said. "That's all. Except you forgot Internal Affairs guys are probably following them two dirty cops around. Glass and Alcantare."

"Okay, them, too. What about Dzekas?"

Cheo thought about that for a moment. "Dzekas is crazy. No question. But you know what, I think he's for real. What you see, that's what he's got."

"So do we keep going?" Pete said.

Cheo looked at the horse across the street and sighed. To his right, the street sloped gently downhill to the Hudson River, and Jersey loomed green and indistinct on the other side. The Bronx was miles away, back over his left shoulder somewhere. Cheo knew that even if he could talk his mother into running away, leaving immediately and going to hide out in her sister's basement, it would only be a matter of time before the same cast of characters came looking for them. "I don't think we got a choice," Cheo said. "We go home now, none of these people will ever leave us alone. I think we gotta do this."

CHAPTER 10

Funny, Cheo thought, lots of people are afraid of the subway, but once he and Pete were back underground, he felt safer. Out on the sunlit Manhattan streets he'd felt too exposed, as though the whole world could watch what he was doing. Down in the tunnels you could only see the other people who happened to be riding in the same car as you, you couldn't see all the buildings or the throngs of people, couldn't feel the energy and urgency of Manhattan, and you didn't need to feel disloyal about comparing those places to your neighborhood in The Bronx. Yeah, life would probably be different if he had come up on these more prosperous streets, if he were not who he was, but what could you do? If you were a city horse you stood in your harness in the street out in front of your horse garage and you waited until it was time to go to work, you probably didn't even dream about grass or whatever because if you'd never felt any underneath your hoofs, all you knew was what you knew.

At least he had baseball.

He and Pete rode the trains for hours, killing time as the afternoon wore on and evening approached. Pete kept a casual eye on where they were and where they were going. Cheo managed to relax after a while, watching the people come and go took his mind off his problems. He watched young girls dressed to impress, ordinary people unremarkable and half asleep, young guys trying to look bad, and once a couple of men in USMC uniform who didn't need to try. Finally Pete got them off the train they'd been riding and they wound up on the L. They got off at the Greenpoint Avenue station and a flood of other riders got off with them. Cheo's anxiety ratcheted up a few notches as they walked through the station and out into the open air.

But Greenpoint was nice.

It looked like it could have been a town all on its own if only it had been plopped down in some other place, it seemed to Cheo that it was only because it occupied one small corner of Brooklyn that he had never heard much about it. He liked the red brick buildings, liked the old fashioned downtown section, liked the parks, green with trees and grass. Pete stopped a Newt Gingrich-looking old lady to ask for directions but she didn't speak English and his Polish was limited to 'hello, how are you, goodbye.' He tried again with more success a block further on. "Straight," the second old lady said, gesturing which way that meant. "Straight up there. Go right on Greenpoint Avenue, take the bridge over the water, and you gonna see." Her right hand fluttered high up over her head. "You gonna see the Kosciuszko Bridge way up inna sky." She nodded, grinning with what teeth she had left. "Kosciuszko. War hero. Come to America to fight. Drive the British out." She nodded again, emphatic. "Kosciuszko. From Poland. Great American. Then you go straight up the hill, you gonna see Calvary. Can't miss."

"Thanks." Pete nodded, distracted as he wrote her directions on the heel of his hand.

The neighborhood deteriorated, it got more and more industrial the further away they got from the downtown section. Soon enough the avenue was lined with old garages and half empty factory buildings. Even the road got worse, beaten and pitted, with cobblestones showing through here and there. The woman was right, though, they did see the Kosciuszko soaring high in the air off to their right, so high it seemed to pass the whole neighborhood by. But Greenpoint Avenue crossed the filthy water of Newtown Creek on a bridge far less grand than the

Kosciuszko. The water beneath the bridge was green and still, you could not see down into it at all, the only sign that it was not simply a wide green swath painted on the ground was the reek drifting up through early evening humidity. Cheo and Pete stopped right at the peak of the bridge's meager rise to look down over. "Guess nobody goes swimming in that," Pete said.

"Yikes," Cheo said. "You think anything could be alive down there?"

"Crabs, maybe," Pete said. "But they'd probably give you rabies if they bit you."

On the far side of the bridge, the bleak industrial landscape rolled on up a shallow hill. The only place that looked open was a warehouse that proclaimed the availability of Hallal meats on a sign over an open truck bay door. Inside, men dressed in flowing Arabic clothing, their faces shiny with sweat, unloaded boxes from a truck. Cheo and Pete stopped to watch for a while but the men inside seemed too worn down to acknowledge their presence. The two boys traded a look of sympathy for the men inside. No matter how bad you think you've got it, there's always somebody who's got it worse.

Cheo nudged Pete. "Check it out," he said, and he pointed up the hill. A couple of blocks up the hill, just before a big green sign hanging over the middle of the street pointed the way to the entrances to the Long Island Expressway, a cop stood in the middle of Greenpoint Avenue, directing traffic. "I think that's the main gate," he said. "That's where you get into Calvary Cemetery. There must be some kind of funeral going on."

"That ain't no funeral," Pete said, squinting. "A funeral is like a whole row of cars following a hearse. That looks more like everybody trying to get into the parking garages at Yankee Stadium all at the same time." It was true, there didn't seem to be any order to the crush of traffic by the gate. The sounds of bleating horns drifted down the hill in the growing dark. "Look at these guys," Pete said, pointing at a few cars rolling slowly down the hill. "They look like they're trying to find parking spots."

Cheo looked at the Asian face of the guy driving the nearest car. The guy slowed and peered down each side street he passed. "Yeah, you're right," he said. "What could be going on? Maybe they're giving away free cheese in the graveyard or something."

"Yeah, free toe cheese, maybe," Pete said. "We can't go in by the gate anyhow, ten cents to a buck that lady is in there watching for us. And Glass and his buddy are up there somewhere too, you could bet on it."

Cheo nodded his head. "Yeah," he said. "The dirty cops. Plus Tasya Gaitanis, and it won't be just her. She still has two guys with her, plus the Jamaican. We gotta go around the back and find a place to hop the fence. Too bad there's no kids that live around here, I bet they would know a good place."

"You think so?"

"If you lived around here, you'd know a back way in. Where else could you hang out? You ain't gonna go down by that disgusting water. You couldn't go fishing in there or nothing."

"What do you think is going on?" Pete said. "What are all those cars doing here?"

"I don't know," Cheo said. "Come on, we passed a street that goes around the back of the graveyard."

"Laurel Hill Boulevard," Pete said, reading the notes on his hand.

Which sounded a lot nicer than it looked. It ran around the back of the graveyard, between an imposing stone wall topped by an iron fence and a row of shuttered, crumbling brick warehouses that stood between the road and the polluted waters of Newtown Creek. The stone wall buttressed the back of the graveyard, it was about twenty feet high, and the surface of the graveyard was even with the top of the wall. Right down the street and high overhead the Kosciuszko loomed in the dark, and the noise of the cars and trucks roaring by was a constant hum. It seemed to Cheo that the whole neighborhood was dead or dying, poisoned, perhaps, by the air drifting out of Calvary or the reek of Newtown Creek. Even the sumac bushes, the cockroaches of the plant world, were stunted and sickly, clinging weakly to life. "Dude," Pete said, looking at the grassy verge at the top of the wall. "Look how high that is."

"Yeah," Cheo said. "All the guys buried up there are six feet under and they're still looking down at us."

"You're creeping me out," Pete said.

"Oh-oh. When we're climbing out, they gonna be looking straight out in between the rocks at you."

Pete looked affronted. "Knock it off, jackwagon," he said. He pointed up. "I see lights up there. And we're a long way from Pelham Parkway."

"It's those people who were lining up to get in, you dope," Cheo said. "It can't be ghosts."

"How do you know?"

"Imagine you was a ghost," Cheo said. "What if you came up out of the ground and all you could see was empty warehouses, highways going by and that horrible water back there? This has to be the worst place in the world to be buried. It's so depressing all you would wanna do is go back down in your grave and go back to sleep, you couldn't even kill yourself because you'd be already dead."

"Yeah, sure," Pete said. "Unless you got hungry and had to come out to eat some brains."

"That ain't a ghost that eats brains," Cheo said, "that's a zombie, and anyhow, you're probably safe either way."

"Very funny," Pete said. "We climbing up or what?"

The wall wasn't hard to climb because the stones were still rounded boulders, piled on top of one another. When they reached the top, Cheo and Pete rested for a minute, they stood there holding on to the bars of the wrought iron fence that stood on top of the stone wall. The graveyard was dotted with moving lights but each light was a lantern, not a ghost, and small knots of people gathered little groups here and there.

"What the hell," Pete said, sounding relieved. "What's going on?"

Cheo shook his head. "No clue." Every day it seemed that the world became stranger, filled with more and more things that he did not understand. "This way," he said. "There's a stone missing over here and we can go under the fence."

They went in, then stopped to watch an old Chinese lady. She was all alone and she was bent over and struggling with a sumac sapling that had sprouted next to a gravestone. She was clearly losing the battle, she was too slight, too frail, and the sumac clung too stubbornly to the dirt. After a moment, she paused to catch her breath and she noticed the two boys watching her. She stared back, unafraid.

"Can we help?" Cheo asked her. "Cause it looks like that thing's gonna kick your butt."

"Don't bet on it," she said.

"Me and Pete can do it," he said. "Let us try."

She nodded and stood aside. Cheo and Pete stepped up, grabbed on and pulled, to no effect. "Cripes," said Pete.

The old lady cackled.

"We'll get it," Cheo told her, and they tried again, but they succeeded only in stripping the outer layer of bark from the plant, exposing the slippery layer underneath.

The old lady stepped back up. "All together," she said. "Grab on. One, two..."

Cheo pulled until he saw spots dancing in front of his eyes. He was about to ease off when he felt the sapling begin to come loose. The others must have felt it, too, and with one last heave they tore the thing out. It let go all at once, dumping all three of them on their butts in the grass.

"Thank you," the old lady said.

"What's up with all the people?" Pete asked her. "What are you guys doing?"

"Qing ming," the old lady said. "Tomb sweeping day."

"Oh my god. Tomb sweeping?" Pete didn't sound happy. "Whose idea was that?"

"Ceremony," she said, eying him defensively. "Very old ceremony. Maybe the very first one."

Cheo looked out across the graveyard. "You're kidding me. That's what all you guys are doing? Pulling weeds?"

She nodded. "Pull weeds, cut grass, put flowers. Some rice, maybe. Burn some money."

"Whoa," Pete said. "Burn money? Are you serious?"

"I show you," she said, nodding. "First I get rid of this." She reached for the sumac.

"I got it," Cheo said, getting up, and he took the sapling over to the fence and chucked it over, down to the street below.

"Not what I had in mind," the old lady said, chuckling, "but, okay."

Pete got up, helped her to her feet. "Look," she said, pointing to a man some distance away. The guy held a flaming piece of paper in his hand. "Burnt," she said, "for the spirits of his ancestors."

"You're serious," Cheo said.

"Not really," she said, and she pulled a wad of papers out of her pocket, peeled one off and handed it to Cheo.

"Oh," Cheo said. "Monopoly money." He turned it over, looked at the picture on the back. "Emperor of Hell," he read. "He doesn't look like a bad guy."

"Emperor of Hell?" Pete said, aghast.

"Good guy," the lady said, shaking her head. "Don't worry." She looked at Pete. "Why you worry? You're too young to worry about that. I got socks older than you."

Pete didn't seem to be buying it. "Emperor of Hell?"

"So this is all for spirits?" Cheo asked her. "Do you believe in them, for real?"

"Who knows?" she said, shrugging. "Maybe. Maybe not." She took the piece of paper back from Cheo and lit the corner of it with a cigarette lighter. "Pay my grandfather's rent, maybe." She cackled, held the paper until it burned down close to her fingers. "Once a year," she said. "Everybody come. Qing ming." She stared at Cheo, wrinkled her face up in puzzlement. "You guys come to help?"

Cheo kicked off a sneaker, retrieved the little red envelope with the key that Pelios had given them and handed it to her. "We gotta find this place."

"Mausoleum," she said, squinting at the key. "Low number. Up by the gate." She shook her head. "Not lucky, this number."

"Great," Cheo said.

"You really believe in spirits?" Pete asked her.

"Who are you?" she asked him, and she poked him in the chest with a bony finger. "Are you this?"

"Am I..."

"Suppose I cut off your hand, which piece is you?"

"The bigger piece," he said.

"Cut off your legs?"

"Um, same answer. I think."

"Cut off your head?"

"Ahhhh..."

"Wrong," she said, and she poked him in the chest again. "You are not this. You are spirit."

"You do believe in spirits," Pete said, shivering.

She shrugged. "Maybe. Who knows?" She handed the key back to Cheo. "Up the hill," she said. "Up by the gate, I think."

"Oh crap," Cheo said, thinking of the Greeks.

"Everybody go home soon," she said, looking around. "You'll be alone, maybe. Thanks for helping. Be careful, that's not a good number. Unlucky." She looked at Pete's ashen face. "BOO!" she yelled, laughing when he jumped back.

"Come on," Cheo said. "We gotta go."

CHAPTER 11

t wasn't rain, really, just a mist hanging in the night air, a damp velvet caress soft on your cheek, a small and polite reminder that you ought to be comfortable up in your bed instead of climbing around in this dark and clammy cemetery. The small family groups seemed to pay no mind to the deteriorating weather, though, they just went about the business of tending to the resting places of their dead. Cheo and Pete headed up the hill right through the center of the graveyard, angling across in the general direction of the main gate.

Pete seemed to be dragging.

"You okay?" Cheo asked him. "You ain't still stressin' about ghosts, are you?"

Pete shook his head. "Not really," he said. "I would be, probably, if there wasn't so many other things to worry about. I don't know if I should be sweating those guys that chased us through the subway station or those two cops."

Cheo nodded. "Or Dzekas," he said. "I don't know if I would rather have him on our side or on theirs."

"I wish we could just go home," Pete said. "But we can't. It's too late for that, isn't it?"

"If these guys don't find what they want," Cheo said, "they'll just come looking for us again."

"Well, that sucks," Pete said. "You still got the key?"

"Yeah, course," Cheo said, shoving a hand into his pants pocket to check.

"Good," Pete said. "Let's go find this place and get it over with." All his thoughts of getting rich seemed to be forgotten. "We get this done and I get back home, I swear to God I'm staying on City Island for the rest of my life, the only time I'm coming back across the bridge is to play in a baseball game."

They stopped when they reached the crest of the hill. The lights of Manhattan lay low in the distance beyond the cemetery main gate, and headlights and the moaning of truck tires echoed from the Long Island Expressway in one direction and from the Brooklyn-Queens Expressway in the other. "The one we're looking for," Pete said, "that old lady said it would probably be up by the gate."

"Yeah. Do you believe..."

Cheo stopped because he heard voices speaking English. He and Pete sunk down in the grass, sheltering in the shadow of one of the more enormous monuments. "Glass is the one you gotta look out for," a man's voice said. "His partner, Alcantare, is not exactly Hello Kitty either, but if you see Glass before I do, especially if he's behind us, I want to know right away."

"I can't believe I got talked into this," a woman's voice said. Cheo finally spotted them, they were a young Chinese couple, the woman carrying flower pots while the man grappled with something in what looked like a large plastic garbage bag.

"What the..." the guy said. "Are you a cop or aren't you?"

"I work in *records*," she said.

"Oh my god," the guy said. "Do you even know how to fire your weapon? Do I have to show you where the safety is?"

"I don't even believe in all this Qing ming crap," she said.

"Are you joking? You don't need to believe in... We just needed an Chinese female officer, and you were the only choice that could get here in time for... You know what, I can't tell when you're busting my chops or what."

"You're not married, are you?" she said. "When in doubt, assume I'm breaking your balls. I bet you don't even have a girlfriend."

"God. Do I need this? Tell me, God, what did I do? How hath I offended thee? Why hast thou afflicted me with this dim bulb? What must I do to atone..."

She laughed then, low and musical.

"All right," he said, lowering his voice. "They tell me that Glass and Alcantare are in a blue Ford van and they're on the Long Island Expressway, headed in this direction. Now I'm gonna be on the parabolic mike and I'm gonna have headphones on, so my peripheral vision is going to be lousy and I need you to watch my back. Try to make sure I don't get shot, okay? And if you see Glass and I don't, especially if he's behind us, you make sure you let me know. Okay? Because we're on our own in here, there's a backup team in case we decide to make an arrest but they're not going to move in unless they get the word from us. From me, actually. Think you can remember all that?"

"I got you," she said. "I got you, baby. But if I break a nail behind this, I swear to God..."

"For crissake! Will you knock it off?"

She laughed that musical laugh again. "Quit worrying. C'mon, Tarzan, let's go." The two of them set out for the main entrance. Cheo and Pete stayed put for a few moments.

"This way," Cheo said softly to Pete. "This way..." He and Pete cut across the grass and ducked around behind one of the small stone buildings.

"Wow" said Pete. "The real cops must be after Glass and Alcantare."

"Yeah," Cheo said. "Nice to know there's someone here that ain't after you and me. I think we should hang out here a little while."

"Good idea," Pete said, and they crouched down in the darkness, up close to the relative cool of the granite wall. They stayed there and watched for a while as the people in the cemetery began finishing up their obligations to the dead and filtering back up to the front gate. There was a small stone building up near the gate, it wasn't a mausoleum, it looked more like a cross between an old-fashioned house and a cathedral but it was built in the wrong scale, it was way too small to function as either. Two men and a woman loitered near the door of a mausoleum a little farther in, opposite the small building, as Cheo watched one of them opened the mausoleum door and they all went inside, closing the door behind them. A moment later a match flared inside a van parked by a hydrant on Greenpoint Avenue, just outside the gate. "Somebody lighting up a number," Pete said.

"Yeah, maybe." A short time later someone got out of the passenger side of the van, tall guy wearing a long coat. When he passed under a streetlight Cheo could see who it was. "Glass," he breathed. They watched as Glass approached the mausoleum.

"Oh crap," Pete said. "So that hadda be them, those three that went inside, they were the ones from the subway station. Tasya and them. They went into that one, can you see the number on it? Did they get there before us?"

"I can't see the number."

Glass stopped by the fence and peered through.

"Why's he just standing there?" Pete said.

"Because he's a cop. He ain't used to sneaking around."

Glass waited there a moment or two and then returned to the van. "He's watching them," Pete said. "If they come out of there carrying boxes or a chest or something, he'll be all over them. Do you suppose that's the right one? The right mausoleum? Because one of them had a key to it."

"No idea," Cheo said. "But if they knew which one had the money in it and they already had a key, why were they messing with me and you? They could have just went right in and took what they wanted."

"Yeah," Pete said. "So if there's no money in that one, what are they doing in it?"

"Beats me," Cheo said.

"I wanna go down for a look," Pete said.

"No, let me," Cheo said. "I'm faster than you."

"No you ain't! Besides, I'm a better sneak than you. Anyway, I don't think they're really looking for me. I think they're looking for you, because you're the one Pelios hooked up with. Stay here."

"No, wait," Cheo said. "Don't do it. Those two in the van are watching."

"Yeah," Pete said, "but they're in a bad spot. I can go straight down over the hill, if I angle over that way a little, that building up by the fence will be between me and them. They'll never see me."

"Wait. I'll come too."

"No!" Pete whispered harshly. "You gotta stay here and keep the key safe!"

"I think this is a seriously bad idea."

"They won't catch me," Pete said. "I'm just gonna get a little closer. If I can hear what they're doing in there, we'll know whether or not they already found the money, because if they did," he said, "then we can get the hell out of here and go home." He sounded like that was what he really wanted.

"What if we get separated?" Cheo said. "What if..."

"If anything happens, run," Pete said. "I'll meet you at midnight, right at the spot where we climbed up the wall. Do you remember where that was?"

"Yeah, but I don't have a watch, you doofus, and neither do you. How you gonna tell when it's midnight?"

"Oh. Yeah. Okay. Well, stay here and I'll be right back. Anything happens, we'll meet back at that same spot, whatever time it is."

Cheo shook his head. "This is nuts."

"Chill," Pete told him. "I'll be right back." Pete slithered down the hill, keeping low, staying in the deepest shadows he could find. Cheo never saw the skeletal white hand that reached out of the dark, wrapped itself around Pete's mouth and dragged him down.

Ashes to ashes, that's what they said, dust to dust. Pete remembered hearing it from a television preacher and it didn't sound so bad when you put it that way. They dug a hole and put you in it, covered you over with dirt and then eventually you turned into dirt yourself. If that was the way it worked, it wasn't so horrible, and maybe in the long run it really did go that way but short term, there seemed to be some intermediary phases a body went through that were pretty awful.

There was no smell, thank God for that much, they had all been dead too long. Inside the mausoleum, the back wall was a kind of bookshelf for dead people, sort of like a honeycomb that had cells with four sides instead of six. Each cell was a long stone cavity intended for a single occupant whose casket would be sealed inside with a stone slab inscribed with the name and particulars of the dearly departed. Inside the Gaitanis mausoleum, however, the stone slabs that had once sealed up the individual cavities had all been smashed and the stone fragments littered the floor. Also spread across the floor were tatters of clothing, shards of bone and bits of what looked like dried skin. Pete was more than reluctant to enter but he was compelled by Dzekas, whose hand was clamped around his shoulder. Pete thought he could probably break free and escape, but there was no point. He was in too deep.

It was no good running away now.

Dzekas stopped in the open doorway. "This place has been searched a hundred times, you know." The three people inside jumped like little kids who'd gotten caught torturing the neighbor's cat.

They made an odd trio. The woman, Tasya, was the most compelling because she had such an abundance of what most men sought. Pete was not immune, he sort of wanted to like her, wanted her to like him back, but she was crazy, she was the worst kind of crazy. Pete had seen enough disordered thinking in his short life and he knew that the sort of insanity that left a person drooling and talking to herself was bad enough, but the other sort, the kind that urged the person out and into desperate service of some lost cause, well that was a lot worse. You couldn't live with that kind of crazy.

She was accompanied by two men. One was her half-brother Vasilios. He seemed older than her but looked weaker, he was pudgy, cowed, subservient, afraid. And oddest of the three, perhaps, or maybe just the guy who stuck out the most was the Jamaican, the guy who had, not long ago, been head of the Black Hand. He had the shiftiest eyes. He was the first to recover from the shock of Dzekas and Pete's surprise entrance. He didn't say anything but he edged away from the other two, eyeing the exit.

"We didn't come here to look," Tasya said, whipping her head about and flinging her long hair back out of her eyes. "We came so I could spit in my father's face." And then she did it, she hawked and spat into an open coffin that had been pulled halfway out of its niche. Pete could not help seeing inside where a skull that had once been human wore dried-out, leathery lips that were shrunken into a gap-toothed, noiseless scream. Tasya reached a hand into the bag she had slung from one shoulder, groping for something. "Do I know you?"

Her pudgy brother stepped forward, eyes widening. "Dzekas? Is that... I mean, ah, is it you? What happened? What happened to you? Everyone thought you were, um, dead..."

"Vassi. How are you." Dzekas grinned his own skeletal smile. "I am a shadow," he said. "One of the Lord's sheeps, passing in the night. I caught this kid hanging around outside. He's one of the little bastards Pelios talked to just before he bought it."

"He's dead, then? Pelios is dead? Are you sure of that?"

"I saw him shot and falling in the river."

Vasilios started to say something else but Tasya silenced him with an open hand. "Does the kid know where it is?" she said, nodding at Pete.

"No, he doesn't. His little friend, who has Pelios's key, got away clean, but I know what you're looking for and I know where you should look."

"Why should I trust you?" she demanded. "I'm not looking to make this a four way split."

"I know what kind of split you'd like to make, Miss Gaitanis. Is that the name you're going by these days?"

She ignored his question. "Why did you come, then?" Her gaze shifted over to Pete. "If Pelios is really dead and that other little turd is gone, then all we have is this one..."

"He can't help you," Dzekas said. "He told me where to look, earlier today, him and his buddy, but they didn't realize that they done it. You could pull out his teeth one at a time and he still wouldn't be able to help you. But I can."

She stared at Dzekas the way a hungry lion stares at a baby goat. "You found it? You found it? Why didn't you just take the money and run? What do you want with us? What's the catch?"

"The catch is that I need a hundred and twenty five grand."

She scowled. "Why? Why that number?"

"I got my reasons. Look, I can't do this myself, I'm too far gone. Soon enough, I'll be just like the old man, there." He nodded at the open casket. "I need you, you need me. What's it gonna be?"

"Tasya," Vasilios said softly. "He's not asking for that much..."

She stood, her suspicions simmering. Pete's gaze wandered. One of the ruined coffins was much smaller than the others and two tiny black-brown feet protruded from the end. Tasya saw him looking. "My baby sister," she said, then corrected herself. "My baby half-sister." She took a step, looked down at the once-white wooden box. "When I was young I used to have dreams where she tried to talk to me."

Pete struggled to find his voice. "On Hart Island," he finally croaked, "sometimes they carry lights down to the shore. Looking for someone to carry them across."

A shadow passed by the open door and Tasya shivered. Dzekas turned and pulled the door most of the way closed, leaving them all in gloom. "I tell you what," Tasya said after a moment. "I'll give you twice what you're asking. Two and a half, but I want the kid."

Dzekas looked over at Pete, then back at her. "Deal," he said. "But I keep him with me until you get back with the money."

"You lousy prick," Pete said.

"Done." Her eyes glittered in the dark. "Tell me what you know."

"It's the eyes," Dzekas said. "That's what Pelios told 'em. It's the eyes that tell you where to look."

"Oh, for crissake! Are you nuts..."

"Maybe. But step outside and look up over the door."

They all scrambled outside to look. Carved into the stone above the door, a gargoyle's unseeing eyes glared out into the night. They all turned as one and looked in the same direction. Off in the distance, at the top of the rise, a single stone mausoleum stood apart from the others, backlit by the lights from the Long Island Expressway.

"That's it," she breathed. "All these years we were so close... Hold him," she said, staring at it. "Hold him right here." She glanced at the Jamaican. "You come with me." She turned to her brother. "You stay with these two. Make sure nobody goes anywhere."

"I think I should come with you two..."

"Don't think, Vasilios," she snapped. "You'll hurt yourself. Look, we don't know for sure whether or not we'll find anything in this next vault, and Dzekas looks like the walk up the hill would finish him off. If we come up empty, he'll be all we have left, so stay here and watch him.

We'll be back." She looked around wildly. "We're gonna need to carry it all out as fast as we can manage..."

Vasilios grumbled but she turned her back on him and stalked away, the Jamaican close behind. Dzekas and Vasilios watched them until they disappeared among the tombstones. "You can't be this dumb," Dzekas finally said. "Tell me, Vassi, that you ain't as stupid as you look right now."

"Shut up," Vasilios said.

"You trust her?" Dzekas sounded incredulous. "Are you... kidding me?" Suddenly he seemed to be struggling for air.

"Shut your face," Vasilios said, sounding angry and scared. "Shut it, or I'll shut it for you."

"Sure you will," Dzekas said. "You know... what she's gonna do, don't you." It wasn't a question. "She's gonna... take the money... slit the Jamaican's throat, and she's gonna... call the cops just as soon as she hits the sidewalk. She's gonna send them... right here."

Vasilios was becoming visibly agitated. He couldn't stand still but he didn't seem to know what to do. "I told you to shut your hole!"

"Yeah, yeah," Dzekas said. "I hope you like prison. They're gonna stick us for the dead... Jamaican, which don't know he's dead yet. You wait and see. You're gonna... do hard time for it. I won't... but you will. Oh, and kidnapping. I forgot about our little friend here." Dzekas closed the door behind him, leaned against it and slid down to a sitting position in the grass. He wiped his forehead. "I loved your father once," he said, "so I'm gonna do... you a favor. Listen to me. There's no money. I checked that building already. Nothing good... is gonna come to nobody out of this, you hear me? The only way... you're walking away from this is if... you walk right now. People are gonna die tonight... I swear it... on my mother's grave."

Vasilios took an uncertain step, then another one, and then he was running, heading for the main gate. Dzekas watched him go and laughed, an awful wheezing sound that ended in a racking cough. "Never did have no guts."

"Are you okay?" Pete asked him. "Let's get outa here..."

"Nah." Dzekas patted the ground beside him. "I don't feel much like walking. Staying... right here."

"But she might come back!"

"Yeah, maybe, but not for a while."

"Is there really no money up in that other mausoleum?"

Dzekas grinned a ghastly smile. "There was. I moved it."

"All by yourself?"

Dzekas cackled. "What did I tell you? I told you there wouldn't be no gold bars. It wasn't nothing like that." He beckoned for Pete to come closer. "There wasn't no money there," he whispered. "The old man didn't leave his dough here. But he had rented storage units all over the state. He left the keys in that building. Each key is taped to a piece of paper, each piece of paper has directions and pass codes and what not. For each storage unit, you need the key and the directions. That's how you're gonna get the money."

"Holy crap," Pete said. "Then it's really real."

"Didn't believe it, did you? Yeah, it's really real, and if you get through this it's gonna change your life, whether you want it to or not."

"Holy crap," Pete said again, and then he shook his head and came back to where he was. "C'mon, let's get you to a doctor."

"Don't worry about me, kid. You gotta go get those papers. They're in a manila file folder. You could stick the whole thing down your pants, under your shirt, and nobody would be the wiser."

"Are they in that building, up where she's going?"

"Not any more." He beckoned Pete closer yet. Pete bent down and Dzekas whispered in his ear.

"That's messed up," Pete said, standing up.

"Only an honest man would say that," Dzekas told him. "Go on, now. You know what you gotta do, you better get going." He coughed again, a horrible, wet, sickening rattle.

"We gotta get you to a doctor..."

"Listen to me, kid. I'm gonna be fine." He looked up into Pete's disbelieving face. "Really. I'm gonna be all right, I got a feeling. You wanna know what I need from you? I need you to get going, go do what you gotta do."

Pete didn't look convinced.

"Listen, maybe it ain't right that it comes to you to do this, but that's the way it goes sometimes. It's your job now, and you're wasting time.

And every no-good rat bastard in this graveyard is gonna be looking for you, so be careful. Go, g'wan. Do this one last thing for me. You promised."

"Are you sure?"

Dzekas nodded once. "I'm good."

CHAPTER 12

The longer he sat and waited, the more Cheo thought sitting and waiting was a dumb idea. He watched the few remaining family groups tending to their rituals, wondered what it must feel like to have someone who'd come out and pull the weeds around the spot where you were buried. He thought about his mother, riding the train from The Bronx to come and make sure there were no sumac trees growing around his grave. The Chinese cops that he and Pete had noticed were not far off, they were struggling with something in the dark but he paid them no mind. This place sucks anyhow, he thought, I would rather wind up on Hart Island, buried along with the rest of New York City's lost souls, and every night I could carry a light down to the water's edge so Pete could look across and see it from City Island, and remember me...

Eventually he stirred, somewhat reluctant to leave his spot, which was now almost completely unlit, but he was worried about Pete, who really should have returned already. It was now too dark to see anything of whatever was going on down at the Gaitanis mausoleum, so he approached carefully, expecting trouble, but everything was still. It was only when he got close that he saw the body lying curled up on its side in front of the door. It couldn't be a homeless guy because there were no garbage bags in evidence, no shopping cart and no cardboard. It was a rare homeless dude who would admit that he really had nothing, because a bagful of old newspapers or empty beer cans or old clothes was generally enough to help you pretend that you weren't a no-good bum two steps ahead of the undertaker, you were merely transporting your stuff to your next home, the location of which you were gonna figure out in the next day or two... It wasn't Pete laying on the ground, either, the body was way too big. He approached with as much care as he could muster, ready to run should the figure leap up off the ground to chase him, but it did not.

It was Dzekas. He looked calm, peaceful, really, like he was sleeping, except his face was gray in the moonlight. After some hesitation, Cheo knelt and nudged him gently on a shoulder but he did not stir, and looked like he would not, ever again. Cheo silently apologized for doubting him because he hadn't been a bad guy, even though he kept telling Cheo and Pete that his sins were scarlet. The guy was wack, no question, but he had saved Cheo and Pete from a pretty awful experience in the subway men's room, and that had to count for something. Of course, if it was God who did the counting, he probably had his own rules for what counted and what did not, and who knew how that worked.

The door behind Dzekas was ajar just enough for Cheo to wriggle through. Once inside he stood completely still until his eyes had adjusted to the gloom, and he stayed just long enough to survey the wreckage inside, and to make sure that his friend Pete wasn't there. Cheo resolved that no one would ever do this to him. When he died, he wanted them to put him in the ground, under the dirt, where the dead belong.

Back outside, he heard approaching voices and he slipped around the corner of the little building and snuck a short distance away, taking refuge in the nearest, darkest spot, praying into the night as he did so, please don't let anything bad happen to Pete, please let him be okay...

"You were supposed to be keeping watch, you moron!" one of the voices said. "Why do you have to smoke that shit all the goddam time? For once in your life..."

"It helps me to concentrate, so get off it."

Two figures came into view. They were Glass and Alcantare, the two cops. "You see? You see? This one is dead, and the rest of them scrammed." He jerked the door open and peered inside. "Gone. If we come up empty this time I'll kill you myself, I swear to God..."

"Shut up, man! Why is everything always my fault? Why do I have to do everything? I don't know why I even bring you into these things, all you're good for is bitching and complaining. There wasn't nothing here to begin with anyhow, if there had been, we'd have seen them leaving with it."

"How do you know? What if they hopped the fence? What if..."

"Their car is parked right on Greenpoint, you idiot. And I'm telling you for the last time, you better quit breaking my balls or I'll..."

"You'll what? Why don't you just shut your trap and help me figure out where they went? Or would that put too much strain on your little pea brain?"

"You know something, I've had just about enough of you. If there wasn't a big, fat payoff at the end of this I'd kick your useless ass right now."

"Oh really."

A moment later Alcantare lay still, face down in the grass. Glass knelt down next to him, glanced around, then hit him twice more with the rock, two hard shots to the back of the head. Just feet away, Cheo shivered in his hiding spot. Life as a rat, he thought, is tougher than it looks. Make one mistake and the other rats are climbing over your dead body trying to reach what you thought you had right in your hands... Glass stood back up, glanced around again nervously before darting away. Cheo watched until Glass was out of sight. There's one rat who ain't heading for the exits yet, Cheo thought. Pelios was right, the dude wants that peanut butter so bad he can't even see the water any more...

Cheo stood up. He could feel it in his pocket, the tiny red envelope with the key inside, and he was sorry that Pelios had ever given it to him. Find Pete, he told himself. Just find Pete so you can both go back to The Bronx, let all the surviving rats kill each other trying to get the money.

God please let Pete be okay.

Pete knew the number on the key! That must be it, Cheo told himself. One of the rats musta grabbed Pete and made him tell, and maybe they won't need the key if they can break the door down. They'll let Pete go once they get inside and find the money because then they won't need him any more.

That's gotta be it.

Find the door this key opens, he thought, and you'll find Pete. Trade the key for Pete and this is all over. Just don't get caught by Glass or any of the other rats before you get there. He edged off in the dark, keeping all of his senses alert. There was a pathway that led up the hill, it seemed clear in the semi-darkness. He reminded himself once again to be careful. Watch out, he told himself. You ain't the only guy sneaking around in this graveyard tonight... He peered at the number over the door of the closest mausoleum, remembering, as he did so, the old Chinese woman he and Pete ran into on their way in. She had seemed ambiguous about whether she believed in spirits or not, not completely sure whether Qing Ming was a useful ceremony or just an old superstition, but she had been very clear that the number on the key Cheo showed her was a bad omen. Cheo felt for it in his pocket again, thinking, nothing good is going to come out of this vault tonight. A smart guy would back off and wait for another, presumably safer, time to do this. But Pete was out there some-where, probably right up this pathway if he read the tomb numbers right, and Pete was his teammate.

You don't run out on your teammates.

Okay, he told himself, but you can't just go stomping up the hill all fat, dumb and happy. You gotta move like a ghost...

He sensed a presence in the darkness, someone was ahead of him, moving carefully up the hill. He heard the guy before he saw him. The guy was not much more than a shadow himself, and he moved like a hunter, a few short steps at a time and then a few moments of stillness, followed by another series of nearly silent movements taking him farther up the hill. Cheo could not get a clear look at the guy.

Or girl. Didn't have to be a guy, it could be that woman, the one who'd killed her friend right outside his super's apartment. Gregory, he remembered her calling him that. Gregory had been the first one to die, no, wait, he'd been the second. Berria, the super, he'd been the first. The guy had just finished selling out his friend Pelios for ten grand but he hadn't lived long enough to spend any of it. Hell, he hadn't even gotten to see it. He'd been the first to die, though, or at least the first Cheo knew about. Who knew how many had died before that?

The guy moved again, couldn't be the woman because he didn't have the long hair. And he moved like a guy, guys just walk different from women, even when they're skulking. Dude made it about fifteen feet further up the hill, stopped in the shadow of another one of those little stone buildings, where he was invisible. Cheo was about to follow when he heard the noise. Someone was coming down the hill, and they were in a hurry.

It was the Jamaican. He was breathing hard, making no efforts to hide his movements, he came stumbling right down the center of the pathway, he looked like it was all he could do just to keep moving. He was holding his side, bleeding badly from a deep gash on his face. He had almost reached Cheo's hiding place when the man Cheo had been following stepped out of the shadows and called softly. "My brother," he said.

The Jamaican whirled, shocked, almost fell as he spun to face the man behind him.

It was Pelios. He did not look like a spirit. He looked like a guy sneaking up the hill in the dark...

"You!" the Jamaican breathed. "You 'posed to be dead, man!" He backed away two more unsteady steps. "They said they seen ya shot! An' fell in tha river, drowned!"

"I'm not quite as dead as they been saying. Looks like she got you good," Pelios rasped, and he limped toward the Jamaican. "Relax, don't worry, I ain't gonna hurt you. She get you anywhere else? Or just the face?"

The Jamaican coughed, spat red on the grass. "One time in na ribs, but my face killin' me, man..."

Pelios came up close, peered at the man. "I seen plenty of cut wounds, believe me," he said. "Take off your shirt. Oh, shit. Okay, listen to me. I know your face hurts bad, but it's the one in the gut that you gotta worry about. If she nicked a lung or got your liver you don't have a lot of time. Go straight on down the hill, out the main gate. There's a fire house right by the gate, they'll help you there. Don't run, you hear me, but don't waste a lot of time, either."

The Jamaican stared at the ground, shaking his head. "Empty bag c'yan stand up on 'is own," he said. "Jus' tell me one t'ing before I run off. 'Ow much?"

"Wad your shirt up and use it to put pressure on that cut on your face," Pelios told him. "That other one's bleeding on the inside, you got to get to the EMT's for that."

"'Ow much? I gotta know..."

"Nothing, man. It was all a lie."

"But..."

"You're wasting time, and you ain't got that much left."

"But that old man..."

"He was a gambler," Pelios told him. "He pissed away his money as fast as he got it. Basketball, ponies, you name it, the bookies got it all."

The Jamaican took a step backward, shaking his head, cursing under his breath. "All fa nuttin," he finally said. "Kill she. Don' let she live. You let she live, she come for us all." He hawked and spat red into the grass of the path, then turned and half stumbled down the hill.

"Yeah, maybe," Pelios said softly. He stood still, watching the Jamaican in the soft reflected glow from the headlights up on the highway. Finally he turned and looked back up the hill. "Come on out, Lefty," he said.

Cheo walked out into the pathway between the tombstones. "You want your key back?"

"You got it?"

"Right here," Cheo said, reaching into his pocket.

"I thought you'd have it rolled up in your sock," Pelios said.

"You had us all figured. Am I right? Me and Pete, those two cops, Dzekas, that crazy Greek female..."

"Dzekas? You met Dzekas? Ain't he a piece of work?"

"Yeah, he was. I think he's dead. He's down by the entrance, laying in the grass right outside that first vault."

"Damn. I would have loved to see him one last time. He was one of a kind," Pelios said.

"No kidding," Cheo said. He was undeterred. "So this all worked out like you planned it?"

"Oh, come on, kid, tell the truth. Ain't this been fun? Ramming around New York City all night? How cool is that? Looking for buried treasure in a graveyard in Queens, tell me how many guys you know ever had a chance to do that."

"Yeah, dude, it was great. You wanna know my favorite part? It was having that sicko in the men's room at the Lexington Avenue station come rollin' up on me and Pete. That was the most fun I had since those Black Hand dickwads beat the crap out of me last summer."

"Sorry, man." Pelios didn't seem too distraught. "How'd you get out of that one? With the sicko, I mean."

"Dzekas."

"You see? It worked out..."

"Yeah. And Dzekas was gonna kill the guy with his bare hands right there in the bathroom. Only reason he didn't was Pete talking him out of it."

"You got through it, that's all that counts. And now we're this close to the money..."

"Tell you what," Cheo told him. "If you help me find Pete, you can keep mine. Me and Pete can go home. I don't think you got that many rats left."

"Yeah, but I believe a man ought to see something good behind all his troubles. You two had 'em coming out of the woodwork! You did an outstanding job, and I wanna make sure you guys get taken care of. What happened to Pete? How did the two of you get separated?"

"Down at the first mausoleum. Pete wanted to sneak down to find out what was happening, and he never came back."

"How long ago was this?"

"I dunno. Just as it was getting dark."

"Pete knew the number on the key, right?"

"Yeah. I was gonna try and find the place. See if he's there."

"Did you look inside the first one?"

"Yeah," Cheo said. "That's when I found Dzekas. And I don't know who those people are they got buried up in there, but I feel bad for them."

"I don't think they're in a position to care. You find anything besides bones in there?"

"No, but Alcantare is in the grass just around the corner."

"The undercover guy? What happened to him?"

"Him and his friend Glass was arguing. Glass got mad and caved Alcantare's head in with a rock. I didn't check him afterwards or nothing, but I think he's probably had it."

"Nobody can do you like your friends. Here's what I'm thinking, Lefty old buddy. I'm thinking you and me, we go camp out in the weeds somewhere up there on top of the hill. This key fits the door to a mausoleum right on top of the hill. Gaitanis paid a buck and a quarter for it about fifteen years ago, just to have someplace to stash his cash."

"A hundred and twenty-five grand for one of these little buildings?"

"Yeah, you see what I'm saying. This ain't pocket money we're talking about, Lefty."

"Are there any more dead guys in this next place?"

"Not as far as I know. But that could change."

"I bet. So you were lying when you told that Jamaican guy that Gaitanis lost all his money."

"He would probably see it that way. Lefty, that man is a gravely sick individual, and he needs to seek medical attention asap. If he hangs around here a minute longer he probably bleeds to death. Besides, you heard him, he was done already, he said so himself. Nothing but an empty paper bag blowing down the hill. Now come on with me, let's go find out what's what."

Cheo didn't move. "I just wanna find Pete."

Pelios turned and came back to him. "Listen, I know it's been a long day, especially for you. You and Pete came through a lot of stuff that no kid your age ought to have to deal with. And I know that you didn't exactly sign up for that. But sometimes things have a way of balancing out. You know what I'm saying? All the things I did when I was younger, I thought I got away with them, but come to find out, I didn't get away with spit. I hadda pay for every single rotten trick I ever pulled. But it balances out to the good sometimes, too. Sometimes when you do the right thing, good comes to you, just not right away. This could still be a very sweet and profitable night."

"For you," Cheo said. "You spent twelve years dreaming this whole thing up, and it wasn't about the money, neither. If it was, you'd be far away, counting it all somewhere. You wanted to kill some rats. That was your game from day one."

"I didn't kill any rats. All I did was give them the excuse to kill each other. You see how they do. You seen Glass do his own partner just a little while ago."

"Yeah."

"Look, I'm gonna make you a promise. I never did that before, did I? I never promised you a thing."

Cheo thought back. "Nuh-uh."

"So here's a promise. I promise you we'll find Pete. And I promise that you two guys will see some good out of all this."

Cheo stared at him.

"What? You don't trust me? Who taught you how to throw a curve, answer me that."

Cheo scowled at Pelios. "Coach says if I throw the curve it'll mess my shoulder up. He says it puts too much torque on the plates in your shoulder and they won't grow right. He says if I don't wait another year I'll need Tommy John surgery by the time I get out of high school and that I'll never play ball again after that."

"Oh for Christ's sake," Pelios said. "Your coach sounds like an old woman."

"Is it true?"

Pelios stopped to consider his answer. "What did I tell you?" he said. "I told you to keep it in your pocket. I told you not to throw it a lot. Didn't I tell you that?"

Then it was true.

"I asked my mother about your rat trap," Cheo said, his scowl still fixed firmly in place. "She says it don't work."

"She ever try it?"

Cheo didn't answer the question. "She says it only works on mice. Mice love peanut butter but rats don't really care about it. She says rats like to eat meat."

Pelios was quiet. "Sounds like a smart woman, your mother."

"So you never cared about how many mice you drowned. This whole time, you only been worried about the rat. That woman, the one that kept on chasing me and Pete, she's the rat. All the rest of them are just mice. But what are you gonna do with her when you catch her?"

Pelios took his time answering. "I been asking myself that question for longer than you been alive, Lefty. I never wanted to believe she was really a rat. I still don't. Funny, how a guy can be so stupid about one thing and so smart about everything else."

"She ain't that special," Cheo said, thinking, Pelios ain't the only guy who can be hard-nosed. "You could do better than her."

"You didn't meet her under the best of circumstances. You don't... When you look at her, you aren't seeing what I see."

"Maybe not," Cheo said. "What would she have did to me and Pete if she caught us? You think she would have stuck us with that little knife of hers?"

"She didn't catch you..."

"She almost did."

"I had my money on you guys the whole time. Lefty, listen to me. We're *this* close. I admit it, okay, I didn't take as good care of you as I maybe should have, but we all made it here in okay shape, didn't we? What do you say we just finish this? Sometimes the only way through is through."

"I never wanted none of this to happen," Cheo told him. "I just want my old life back."

"It doesn't always work out that way, Lefty."

"Me and Pete got a game on Saturday. That's what I care about. I wanna be there to pitch, and I want Pete there to catch me."

Pelios looked up the hill. "I hear you, Lefty. I hear you. Let's go make this happen, okay? Then we'll get you and Pete back home."

CHAPTER 13

When they reached the top of the hill there was no one around. Cheo hung back, cautious, but Pelios put a hand on his shoulders and urged him on. "She's here," he said, leaning over, his voice hushed. "She's watching, bet on it. Our play is to walk on in and let her come to us."

Cheo complied reluctantly.

Pelios walked up the mausoleum like he owned it. It was much newer than the Gaitanis family vault, the exterior walls were made of clean, smooth polished granite and the door was a heavy black iron affair with no graffiti on it. Pelios took the little red envelope out of his pocket and opened it. He shook the key out, dropped the envelope on the ground and opened the door.

My mother would give you a smack on the head for that, Cheo thought.

He heard a noise behind him.

He turned and she was there, maybe fifteen feet away. She was dressed like she was going to a club: skin-tight spandex below, black tee shirt above. She carried a black bag over one shoulder, and when she moved, her long black hair rolled like waves on the sea. Cheo could hear his mother's voice in his head asking if she wasn't a little old for all that mess, but he kept that to himself. He jabbed Pelios and pointed back at the woman.

Pelios pretended to be surprised. "Tasya Gaitanis," he said, one hand holding the door open. "How nice to see you."

"You must hate me," she said, in an adult version of a little girl's voice. You gotta be kidding me, Cheo thought. Did she actually think that was gonna work on a guy like Pelios?

"How could I hate you?" Pelios said. "You gave me the defining moment of my youth."

Oh my god, Cheo thought. It *is* working. I can't believe it... This guy is blind, he can't see what she really is. It's like this woman put a spell on him. He wondered if there was some way he could shine a light on her, some way to help Pelios see what was right in front of him.

"Besides," Pelios continued. "No one twisted my arm. I made my own choices."

"Don't pretend," she said. "I'll bet you had lots of women, both before and after me."

"Nobody like you. Would you like to come inside?"

I'm gonna gag, Cheo thought.

She didn't answer but she strode across the space between them.

Cheo shrank back.

She stopped, held out a hand to him. "Lefty," she said. "I'm sorry if we frightened you, earlier today. That was not my intention. Truce?"

Bullshit, Cheo thought. "Yeah. Yeah, sure." He didn't shake her hand, he didn't want her touching him.

Pelios pushed the door open wide. "Come into my parlor, said the spider to the fly." He smiled at her as she walked past him. Her eyes glittered.

This one is nuts, Cheo thought. He reached back for that most ancient of survival maxims: keep your mouth shut and stay by the door. "I know how much I owe you," she said to Pelios, still using her baby doll voice. "I'll never forget what you did for me."

"Why did you kill him?" Pelios asked her.

"How can you ask me that?" she said, sounding like she was wounded, struck to the heart. "You knew what he made me do to survive. And he was my father... He made me crawl! He forced me to grovel." She sniffed, seemed to struggle to control her emotions, to keep from crying. Cheo looked at Pelios, who was melting like a Popsicle in August. She swallowed. "He was an awful man. He humiliated me."

Pelios stiffened his shoulders and seemed to rally a bit. "You had a choice. You could have walked away. You could have been anything you wanted to be."

"Your family is supposed to be there for you, Lazur." She's not hearing anything Pelios is saying, Cheo thought. She's not interested in logic. She ain't gonna win by making sense. She's gonna beat him with those tight pants and that sweet thing act. She's not looking for the decision, either, she's going for the knockout. "They're supposed to guide you. They're supposed to care about you. They're supposed to be on your side."

Pelios might have been ahead on points but she was hitting him where he was soft. "I hear you. But at some point... If you're not getting what you need from your parents, at some point, doesn't it become your job to take over? To take care of yourself?" His voice was losing its tone of confidence and conviction.

"You know what I was to him?" she said, sounding like her heart was broken. "I was nothing but a rhetorical point. An argument for corporal punishment. Or for birth control. He never felt anything for me. Nothing but contempt. And when he found out you cared about me, he tried to poison you against me." She looked around the empty mausoleum. "I'm not sorry I killed him," she said. "I found the gun in his coat pocket, and when he came out of my mother's bedroom I held it right up against his forehead. You know what he did? He laughed at me. He said I would never amount to anything. He said I would never be anything but a whore, just like my mother." Her chest heaved and her face grew red as she relived it. "What should I have done? What would you have done?"

Pelios said nothing.

"I do regret that you had to pay the price for what I did, but my father was a pig, and I have never missed him. Not for a single heartbeat." She stared at Pelios, and even from his position over by the door, Cheo could feel the power of her hold over the guy. "I know you loved me once, Lazur. And I promise you I will never forget for one second what you did for me. I never could have survived in prison. I know that now."

"So what next," Pelios said.

"Is it here?"

"His money? Yeah, it's here," he said. He didn't take his eyes off her. Cheo was watching her, too, but he wasn't spellbound, like Pelios. He was suspicious.

She looked down at her shoes. "What about it?" she said. "Are you going to do what he did? Are you going to make me crawl?"

"No."

Cheo looked over his shoulder, saw a short figure walking up the hill. It was Pete, and he was walking funny, kind of stiff and bow-legged the way Yo boys walk when they're trying to keep their pants from falling the rest of the way down. He thought about taking off but something told him it wasn't time yet. Besides, he was getting the beginnings of an idea. Maybe there was a way to help Pelios see what he, Cheo, saw...

Pelios was talking. "I just want to hear it from you. Where do you and I go from here? I paid a high price to get to this point. I really would like an answer."

Pete walked up and stood behind Cheo in the open doorway, but neither Tasya nor Pelios paid him any attention. They were locked onto one another, two cats who hadn't decided whether to fight or kiss and make up. Pete had something tucked into his pants, under his shirt, that's why he was walking funny. He pulled it out, leaned forward and whispered in Cheo's ear.

Cheo shook his head no and mouthed something back.

"You could never trust me," Tasya said softly. "And I could never stop being afraid of you. I know what you really are. Do you think you could live like that?"

Cheo reached behind his back, felt Pete press something into his hands.

Pete melted away.

"So you're just going to walk away from me tonight. Right here," Pelios said.

"Make a fair split with me," Tasya told him. "And go your way. I'll go mine. And someday... Someday maybe I'll find you. For now, I think that's the way it has to be..."

Give it a try, Cheo thought. Why not? "Bleah," he said, standing there with his hands behind his back. "I think I wanna hurl."

Pelios glanced at him, a spark of amusement in his eye. Tasya half-turned but did not look at Cheo. "Why are you still here?" she said.

"I wanna see if this numb-nuts is really gonna buy this baby-doll act of yours," Cheo said.

She twitched and he almost took off, but she stayed where she was so he stood his ground. "Lefty," she said, "please. I know you can't understand what we're going through, but this is hard enough already. Please? For me..."

"He's immune," Pelios said. "You're wasting your time."

"How do you know?" she said, whirling back to him. "What's the difference between him and you, other than his age? He's got the same glands. Why should he be..."

"He's tougher than I am, for one thing. And I'm beginning to think he might be smarter. I keep on looking for the missing ingredient, if you know what I mean. Something I could pour all over myself, and it would make me whole."

"Can we please get on with this?"

"Something that would cure me. Like money, or strength, or street cred. Something that would finally make me okay. You know, something that could get me past that barrier... For a long time I thought it was going to be you. But Lefty, see, here's the thing about Lefty, he doesn't want anything from either of us. What drives him isn't anything you can give him, or take away from him, either. What he cares about is something he wants to be, not something he wants to have. That's why you've got no hold on him. Unlike, for example, me. I understand the concept, but I'm not there yet."

"Christ," she said. "You want me to beg? Okay, I'm begging you." She looked around wildly. "Where is it? For the love of God..."

"All right," he said. "It's up there." He pointed up, where the wall ended about three feet over their heads, the wall where you sealed your dead relatives inside their individual granite cells. "What you're looking for is a manila folder. Each piece of paper inside it has a key taped to it, and there's a different set of directions and a different name for each key. Some of them open storage units, and some of them are for..."

"I get it, I get it," she said. "Lift me up."

He laced his fingers together to form a step. She put a hand on his shoulder and he hoisted her up. She grabbed the top of the ledge and peered over. "There's nothing up here."

"Dude, you ever notice?" Cheo said, thinking, I got her now. "She's getting those flappy things that hang under her arms, like my fat aunt from Jersey's got."

Pelios grunted, his amusement draining the strength from his arms. He lowered her abruptly back to the floor. "Listen, kid," Tasya said, glaring at Cheo.

"Of course it's up there," Pelios said. "Out of the way, let me look." He flexed on his one good leg and jumped. Cheo thought it wasn't possible but Pelios did it, made it all the way up to the top of the ledge and held himself up with his forearms. "But it was right here!" he said. "What the..." He turned, his face drained of color, saw Cheo stuffing a fat manila folder down into the back of his pants, the same way Pete had carried it up the hill. "Lefty! You little..."

Tasya whirled and stared at Cheo.

"You gettin' them old lady wrinkles around your eyes, too," Cheo said. "You looking pretty tired. You been getting enough sleep?"

She grabbed for something in her bag and lunged in his direction but Pelios jumped down behind her. He landed awkwardly but still got a handful of her hair. She whirled, her knife flashed in a long glittering arc, opening a deep cut on Pelios' arm. He let go and sagged back, his face wide in disbelief as his arm bloomed red. She turned, stared at Cheo with a face full of hate, but when she made her move Pelios still managed to get a hand on one of her ankles. She lurched out of his grasp but tripped and fell face down on the floor. The knife flew out of her hand, right out past Cheo's face to land in the grass outside.

Cheo laughed. "Told you she was the rat," he said, and then he turned to run.

CHAPTER 14

Run or hide?

It bothered Cheo, for a heartbeat, that there wasn't another choice but in that same eyeblink of time he knew that he had to be smart... The trick to getting buried treasure, Cheo thought, isn't really digging it up, although that part had been tough enough. No, the trick, really, was getting away. Living long enough to spend some of the cash. The path to the cemetery exit lay before him, paved, relatively straight, clearly visible in the growing dark. Is the easiest answer always the best one?

Maybe not.

Laurel Hill Boulevard lay off to his left, down the hill past the gravestones and monuments. It was the way he and Pete had come and Cheo knew, more or less, what lie in that direction. And the other way, off to his right, the Long Island Expressway stood on spindly green legs in the distance beyond the cemetery fence. Cheo dodged right, instinctively choosing the unlikeliest of his options.

Tasya was not far behind him.

She flew out of the mausoleum, but she stopped when she reached the path that led to the exit, eyes wild as she searched for the prey which had, just moments ago, been within her grasp.

Glass stepped out of the shadows. "Stop right there," he snarled. "Don't move."

Tasya whirled to face him. "You idiot!" she hissed.

He pointed his pistol at her. "Do you want to live? Do what I say or you're dead."

Cheo crouched a short distance away and watched, motionless. Glass might appear to have the upper hand, but Cheo decided he would still put his money on Tasya because she was truly mad and he figured her insanity would defeat the pistol sooner or later, and besides, Glass' sense of self-preservation would give her the opening she needed...

Except it didn't play out that way.

"GLASS! DROP THE GUN!" It was the Chinese guy, the male half of the couple who Cheo and Pete had noticed on their way up the hill. "POLICE! PUT THE GUN DOWN! NOW!" The Chinese cop had been carrying a parabolic microphone, he dropped it in the grass, tore his headphones off and reached for his weapon. "GLASS! YOU'RE UNDER ARREST! DROP THE WEAPON!"

Glass turned to face him, bringing his weapon to bear on the man, whose pistol was still holstered at his waist. Dude, Cheo thought. You blew it. You had to know you were gonna need that gun, God, this can't be happening...

The other half of the Chinese couple stepped out of the darkness. Glass started to swing his gun in her direction, there was a hitch in his motion as he reconsidered but he was in too deep, God, Cheo thought, the guy is gonna do it, he's gonna try and kill them all.

The gun in her hand barked twice, sounded like someone hammering a nail inside an empty house.

Glass fell to his knees, his face a mask of rage and frustration, he screamed as he tried to decide who to kill first but the Chinese cop chose for him. Her pistol barked twice more. Glass went over backwards, blood staining the center of his chest a deep red. He cried out one last time but this time it was the defeated wail of a man who finally realized that he'd made one mistake too many.

Cheo maxed out, he'd had enough. He bolted, he flew down the hill, heading for the main gate.

The two Chinese cops seemed momentarily stunned, in shock at the violent passing of another human being right before their eyes. Tasya, Cheo knew, would not be subject to any such limitations. Catlike, she pelted down the hill behind him, coming hard, ignoring the shouted warnings from behind her. Cheo felt nothing but exhilaration as the main cemetery gate got closer and closer. It was a relief, in a way, because now all of the guesswork and sneaking around was over.

He only had one card left to play.

To his right, lights from a police cruiser stabbed at the Queens night with blue and red daggers of light. They were over on the far side of the highway, coming up the westbound service road and headed in his direction. Too far away to help, Cheo thought, or to screw things up either. For better or for worse, he was on his own.

She almost got him.

When he burst through the main gate out onto Greenpoint Avenue he felt the tips of her claws brush the back of his shirt but he juked left and she missed, she might be as fast as he was but she couldn't turn as quick and like a runner who slides past the base and gets tagged out she slid across the avenue and banged into a parked car on the far side. Cheo, laughing, headed down the hill on Greenpoint, back down past the fire station. He wondered briefly if the Jamaican had made it. Despite thinking the dude was a bad guy, Cheo hoped he'd be okay. There were guys like him all over the neighborhood, get rid of one and another one will pop up to take his place. What was the point of hating them?

He didn't dare to slow down long enough to turn to see how close Tasya Gaitanis was to catching him. Down on the next block, the truck pulled out of the Hallal Meats warehouse that he and Pete had noticed on their way up the hill just hours ago. It was a typical city truck, a beat-up Korean cabover carrying a ten foot box body that was thickly covered with gang tags, but the truck was small enough to negotiate city streets and short enough to almost be parkable. It turned onto the avenue in front of Cheo and accelerated, belching out a cloud of eau de diesel fuel. Cheo leaned down the hill and put on a last burst of speed, running, for a moment, faster than he really could. He knew if he kept it up too long he would wind up sprawled on his face on the street but he did it anyway and he managed to get a hand on the grab handle next to the truck's roll-up door, and with a final leap he was riding instead of running. He yanked himself into a sitting position on the truck's narrow tailgate.

She had only been steps behind. She screamed in frustration as the truck slowly pulled away, increasing the distance between her and her intended meal. Cheo laughed at her again, making her madder than ever but she couldn't keep pace with the truck. She pulled up and stopped. He peered around the corner of the truck to see the traffic light on the next corner turning red but the driver merely slowed, then blew through the traffic light and kept going. Cheo's exhilaration was short-lived, though, because when he turned back around he saw Tasya pulling some woman out of a big black SUV, throwing her to the ground and then jumping in behind the wheel.

His luck held, barely, because the Hallal Meats truck driver was in a big hurry. Maybe the warehouse had been his last stop, Cheo thought, maybe the guy had had a long day too, maybe he wanted to dump this stupid truck back where they parked it so he, too, could go home. The guy didn't head through the congested neighborhood of Greenpoint, either, instead he slithered expertly through the sparse nighttime traffic and took the on-ramp to the Brooklyn-Queens Expressway.

Tasya was not quite keeping up, but she had not given up, either. She was a block and a half behind, roaring to catch them but the truck jockey was a professional driver and she was not, in her haste she side-swiped a couple of parked cars, bounced off and broadsided a car going the other way, which slowed her down a bit. Still, she left the wreckage of the other cars behind her and made it to the on-ramp, though some distance behind Cheo and the truck.

Once on the highway Cheo's truck sped up even faster, making for an uncomfortable ride for Cheo. He had to hang on to the grab handle with both hands to keep from sliding off the steel tailgate, which had been polished smooth by untold thousands of freighted boxes sliding on and off the truck. The truck slowed a bit as it approached the steep slope of the Kosciuszko Bridge but right at the peak of the bridge the driver jerked the truck out into the center lane and got around the limo driver who had been impeding his progress. He sped down the other side. About fifty yards back, Tasya was leaning on the SUV's horn, trying to bully her way through the traffic but the horn didn't buy her much, New

York City's drivers are generally both in a hurry and territorial, therefore unimpressed by horns. Yeah, buddy, we know you're in a rush, so is everybody else, take a freakin' number...

Cheo began to try to calculate his chances. Maybe the guy will lose her, he thought. Maybe I won't fall off and get squashed. Maybe this will all work out after all... He felt the truck change directions as the two left lanes split from the expressway and headed for the Williamsburg Bridge, which would take them into Manhattan. The approach to the bridge resembled a roller-coaster, rising up and falling back to the ground sharply, not so fun when you were clinging to the bumper of a vehicle that was not known for its handling abilities. There was one red light where the driver stopped briefly and the black SUV Tasya was driving, which now had wisps of steam rising around the hood, gained ground rapidly. Cheo was preparing himself to jump down and run for it but his truck driver found a path to daylight and eased on past the cars waiting for the light to change and went through.

Tasya stayed close behind. Cheo could see her through the cracked windshield glass, her face unnaturally white and her black hair all crazy. Seeing her stare at him, Cheo waved, grinning when he saw her grinding her teeth in frustration.

The roadway began to climb.

There are people who say that each useful thing must possess, as a function of that usefulness, its own particular beauty. The Williamsburg Bridge, a rusting, spidery steel skeleton spanning the swift and treacherous waters of the East River, is proof that some useful things are just butt-ugly. Upriver from the Williamsburg, the bridge variously known as the 59th or the Queensboro has a certain magic and majestic elegance, while downriver the Manhattan Bridge wears its ragged blue-collar pride without apology. And, of course, just downriver from that stands the Brooklyn Bridge, the love child of the artist, engineer and visionary named Roebling. It is as famous, as recognizable around the world as any movie star, now or ever. But it would take a true loser to ever sing a love song about the Willy B.

Cheo was conscious of none of that as he clung to his slippery perch.

He was concentrating on the fact that his ride was slowing down, and that Tasya Gaitanis, in her stolen and now half-wrecked SUV, was close behind, on fire for her chance to tear him in half.

Cheo Hernandez was not afraid.

Okay, yeah, maybe he was. But could Tasya Gaitanis deliver a fastball, recover her balance, come down off the pitcher's mound and field a perfect bunt on the third base side of the infield, then turn and fire a strike to the only place where the streaking second baseman could catch it in time to nail the lead runner?

He thought not.

Could Tasya Gaitanis outrun the goons from the T-Mac Nine crew if she happened to walk through their retail spot on the corner on her way home from school and spooked out some feeb from Jersey who, instead of completing his transaction, jumped back into his car and fled?

Not on her best day.

Traffic slowed even more, and then the truck jerked to a stop.

Cheo jumped down, paused long enough to jam the manila folder back down under his belt.

Tasya Gaitanis slammed the gearshift lever on her stolen SUV into park. "Lefty!" she shrieked. "This is not funny any more..."

He was already running past the startled driver of the Halal truck, up in between two lanes of motionless vehicles. The drivers who were now mired behind the stolen SUV, seeing Tasya desert the vehicle, began to bleat their horns in loud and plaintive protest. She ignored them, she had eyes for Cheo and for the riches jammed under his belt, nothing more. Cheo glanced back over his shoulder.

He knew he could not outrun her.

He looked around as he ran, considering his chances. She was between him and Brooklyn, and he was still a long way from Manhattan. She was bound to catch him before he could reach the other end of the bridge. Not good.

He could only think of one other option.

He dodged left to the railing, grabbed the steel bones of the Willy B and began to climb. He knew it was stupid, but he felt the adrenaline bubbling in his blood and he was possessed of that momentary form of immortality available only to a thirteen year old who has been running and fighting his whole life. Maybe tomorrow he would trip and break his neck but on this night, nothing would touch him.

"Lefty! Stop!" And then she was climbing, too, but she was not immortal, just crazy.

He reached the main cables, the fat ones that arced from the top of one spindly metal tower, down almost to road level and then back up again to the top of the other tower. Here, at the bottom of the arc, it was almost too easy. There were two smaller guy wires that ran chest high just above the big cable, they served as railings for the hardhats who had to work on the bridge. Cheo climbed up and stood on top of the main cable. He put a hand on one of the guy wires and began walking backward as he watched Tasya climb.

She glanced up. "Lefty!" she cried.

"That's not even my name," he told her.

She paused for a second, exasperated. "What difference does that make?"

He kept backing up. He figured she would make her move as soon as she got onto the fat main cable, she would want to catch him down near the bottom, before it got too steep. "Yeah, I know," he said, and he kept moving backward. "You don't care what my name is. And you don't care about Pelios, neither. Only yourself."

"Lefty, please! Do you have any idea what you're carrying?" She was almost there. "I don't even want it all... Why don't we split it? You and me. Just stop. Stay there, and, and... we'll each take half. You can keep some of the pages, just jam the rest of them into a crevice, right there where that other cable comes up, and I'll take them and go away..."

"What about Pelios?" he asked her. "What about Pete?"

"Screw them!" she shouted, rage flooding into her face. "They're not here! We are! Just do what I say and we can both walk away from this! I don't want anyone else to get hurt!"

"Yeah, right," Cheo said. "I know what you want. You wanna chuck me right off this bridge into the river. Even Pelios knows what you are now. And you will never catch me."

She vaulted up onto the cable. "I gave you your chance, Lefty," she snarled. "It's on you, now." She went for him.

Cheo turned and scrambled up the cable, which was getting steep in a real hurry. A couple of seconds later he heard her shriek and he turned to look. She must have slipped, she was hanging on to one of the guy wires with both hands and her feet were dangling, scrabbling to get her back up on the main cable. Cheo looked down for the first time. Lose your balance here, he thought, and you'll fall all the way to the roadway and kill yourself, and that's if you're lucky. If you aren't, you could fall all the way down to the river, what those long, horrifying seconds would feel like was something he didn't want to contemplate. Tasya got her feet back under her but her confidence was shaken, her eyes were wild and her chest heaved as she fought to catch her breath. She's human after all, Cheo thought, because she's feeling something... Fear, in this particular instance. Cheo knew all about fear, had known as far back as he could remember.

"Lefty..." She stood back up, her legs shaking. "Lefty, please..."

Maybe that's it, Cheo thought. Maybe that's what Dzekas was trying to tell us. Maybe it's feeling something that keeps you from being another one of the animals. Maybe it hadn't been baseball after all that had given him hope, and life. Maybe it was just that he loved it. Maybe it was that feeling he got when he was pitching for his team, or even just listening to the Yankees on his radio. Even up here high on this dirty ugly rusty bridge he felt a pang when he thought of his glove and his baseball, waiting for him safe under his bed up in The Bronx. Maybe caring about something was what got you through the day without wanting to kill someone, or yourself.

She was gathering herself to make another charge but her heart wasn't in it, not like before. Something told him she wouldn't go through with it. He could hear a helicopter somewhere in the distance, blades going whap, whap, whap. Sirens sounded, far away, but you can always hear sirens in NYC if you listen hard enough, cops always seem to be in a hurry to get where they're going. She looked at him, pleading silently, praying to whatever god it was that ruled her heart.

It worked after all, Cheo thought, the rat just fell into the bucket and now she knows it's over, she knows she's gonna drown... She fooled him, though, she had another run in her and he had to flee up higher, climbing more than running this time because of the arc of the cables. They were both high up over the roadway now and an unthinkable distance from the cold water below. She slipped again, he heard her shriek but he went on to get what felt like a safe distance away before he turned around. She was hanging on to the guy wire, like before.

Manhattan glittered at Cheo's back, hard and bright. Brooklyn twinkled to his right, softer somehow, friendlier, and Queens lay sleeping in the distance. The chopper seemed louder, and airplanes circled silently in the dark sky overhead. Cheo wondered how many people had gotten to stand where he stood right now, to see what he saw.

Tasya was still hanging on the guy wire. It was over now, he knew it and now she did, too. Cheo sat down on the main cable and pulled the manila folder out of his pants. He took a sheet of paper out at random, wadded it into a ball. "You still want this?" he said. He threw it at her but she couldn't let go long enough to catch it, it bounced off her and sailed away into the night.

"You idiot!" she screamed. "You moron! That could have been a million dollars!"

"You can't handle the fastball," Cheo told her. "Pelios was crazy for you. You so stupid, all you hadda do was be nice to him. If you asked him, he woulda gave you everything."

"It was never his to give!" she screamed, her voice cracking. "It was mine!"

Far below her, flashing cop lights began working their way through the simmering mess of vehicles jamming the roadway, and the helicopter blades were much closer now. "They gonna put you away for stabbing that guy Gregory," he told her. "Money ain't gonna do you no good."

"How... How do you..."

"I seen you do it," he said.

"They won't believe you," she told him. "Those are mine, and I can prove it..." She had her feet planted firmly back on the cable now.

"They don't have to believe me," he said. "They'll find Gregory's blood on them shoes you had on. Because I know what you're like. I know you kept them shoes."

She looked like she had been slapped in the face.

He wadded up another piece of paper. "No!" she shrieked, but he threw it anyway. She made a grab for it and missed. "Why are you doing this?"

"Curve ball," he said. "Can't catch the deuce, neither."

"Miss!" It was a faint voice from far below. "Miss! Hold on! Don't do it! Let us help you! We're coming to help you!"

"You don't know anything!" she screamed. Suddenly she was in the center of a blinding sun. It was a police chopper, and its searchlight split the night, lighting her up. They must have cameras on the bridge, Cheo thought, but they haven't noticed me sitting here, they think she climbed up here to jump, and why anybody would want to do that, he couldn't understand. But then, there was a lot he didn't understand...

"You want this?" he asked her, holding out the folder. "Might buy you a better lawyer..."

She stared at him, transfixed.

"Miss! Hold on!"

He tossed it, chucked the whole thing, aimed it a little bit out towards Brooklyn, she sucked in her breath and made a grab for it but the folder opened and then the wind got it, the papers exploded into a ball, the wind sending them flying everywhere, she might have gotten one or two of them but then she was too far below to reach the rest of them because flesh and bone fall much faster than the illusion of wealth. She twisted slowly, graceful as she flew through the air until she caromed off the steel just above the roadway and ragdolled the rest of the way down to the river.

The spotlight followed her down.

The papers fluttered out into the darkness.

Support cables ran from the fat main cable straight down to the roadway far below. Feeling now somewhat less than immortal, Cheo lowered himself carefully until he had his legs wrapped around one of the support cables and then he slid down slowly. He was vastly relieved when he reached the roadway, a little shaken, even, and he trotted over to the Manhattan side. There was a harbor patrol boat coming upriver and the helicopter shone its beacon at the river's surface, looking for Tasya. Cheo slipped away unnoticed into the night.

CHAPTER 15

Cheo could not remember ever being in another place so brightly lit. It was King's County Hospital, that's what the sign over the entrance proclaimed. Everyone inside the place seemed to be in a big hurry to get somewhere, all except the security guard by the door. "Where you goin," the guy said.

Cheo hoisted the brown paper bag in his left hand somewhat awkwardly. "Bagels," he said. "For some guy named…" he consulted the slip of paper he held in his right hand. "Pilios? Peelios? Something like that."

"Yeah? I don't remember seeing you before. Where's the regular kid?"

"How would I know?" Cheo said. "Dude, they're bagels. From the deli. I'm supposed to deliver them." The guy didn't look convinced. "Look, it's gonna cost two hundred bucks for baseball camp this summer and my mother ain't got it. Gimme a break, willya?"

The guy looked at him a moment longer. "Okay, let's get you a pass."

There was another guy in the room with Pelios, an old guy who had the bed closest to the door. He was staring vacantly out into space but he seemed to come out of it when he saw Cheo walk through the door. "I hurt," he said.

Pelios looked over at Cheo. "Lefty!" he said.

"I hurt," the man said again.

Cheo stared into the old man's watery blue eyes. "Sorry," he said.

"I don't think it means anything," Pelios said. "I don't think he remembers how to say anything else."

Cheo fished a bagel out of his paper bag and handed it to the old man, who took it with a shaking hand. "Sesame," Cheo told him. "With butter." The old man looked at the bagel in his hand as if it was the first one he had ever seen.

Pelios had an odd look on his face. "You are something else, you know that, Lefty? So she didn't get you, I take it."

"Nah-uh."

"How'd you get away from her?"

Cheo shrugged. "Some days you play the ball, some days the ball plays you. How you feeling? You okay?"

"I hurt," the old man said.

"When she cut me," Pelios said, "she didn't hit anything real important."

"You sure? Cause you looked like she was stabbing you right in the heart."

Pelios cracked a smile. "What there was left of it."

"You sorry she's gone?"

Pelios' smile disappeared. "You know what? There seem to be some cuts you don't get better from..."

"This oughta make you feel better," Cheo said, and he lifted up the left side of his shirt and fished out some papers he had tucked under his waistband. Pelios eyes went wide when he saw them, and he motioned Cheo over closer and took the papers from him carefully, as though someone had handed him a newborn baby. He leafed through the top half dozen sheets, looking at the numbers written there.

"How... How did you make the split?" he said, his voice even hoarser than normal.

"Pete did it."

Pelios looked befuddled.

"You know, eenie-meanie. One for me, one for you, one for him, and like that."

"There are numbers on all these pages," Pelios told him. "There's like a running total for how much is in each location. You guys didn't try to balance them out or anything like that?"

Cheo took a look. "Yeah, we seen those," he said. "Pete was trying to keep track, but after a while it got too confusing. So, you know, what the heck. Some for you, some for me, some for him."

Pelios held his chest with both arms while he laughed.

"You okay with the way we did it?"

Pelios held himself tighter and kept laughing. "Yeah," he finally said. "Yeah, why not. It's all good."

"What are you gonna do when they let you out of here?" Cheo asked him.

"No idea," Pelios said. "But if I ever grow up I wanna be just like you."

A few days later, Cheo and Pete sat on a stoop across the street from a store-front church on Bedford Avenue in Brooklyn, waiting. There was no telling how much trouble they were going to be in once it was discovered they had decided to go on yet another excursion, but Pete had made a promise and Cheo felt bound by it as well. "What do you figure this guy looks like?" Cheo said.

"I dunno," Pete said. "But he said he might be a little late."

"Too bad about Dzekas."

"Yeah," Pete said. "He musta known he was near the end, he was popping them pills like they was M&M's."

"How did he figure out where Gaitanis hid the money? You never told me."

"Pelios said the eyes would tell you where to look, remember that? Well, there was a gargoyle carved into the stone just above the doorway of that mausoleum that Tasya and them broke into, and the thing was looking right up the hill, right at that second one, the mausoleum that didn't have no dead people in it yet. After we got out of the subway when we was at that coffee shop in Manhattan, we told Dzekas about the eyes, you remember that? So he left us there in Manhattan, he took a cab out to the graveyard and he looked. He found that folder and he broke into the gravedigger's office, which was that little building by the gate, and he left it right on the desk."

"How did he know it would be safe there?"

"Nobody had went into that building for years, everything in there was covered all over with dust."

"So he told you to go and get it."

"Yeah. He even told me which window you could open. Was he dead when you seen him?"

"I thought he was." Cheo's voice was quiet. "I could have said good-bye or, you know, sorry or something, but I didn't, I just left him there. The ambulance guys found him and the paper said he died at the hospital."

"He was probably sleeping," Pete said, sympathetic. "It's better you didn't wake him up."

"Yeah, I guess. Do we know what kinda car this guy drives?"

"No."

Across the street, a battered Toyota Tacoma pickup truck double-parked in front of the church and a tall thin Black guy dressed in the green and yellow colors of the New York Sanitation Department got out of the truck and went into the liquor store next door. "Good thing you took that extra folder out of the gravedigger's office. What was in that one that you gave to me?"

"It said 'Openings, '04' on it. It was just the work orders they gave to the guys that had to dig new holes when they had a new dead guy to bury."

"That was pretty smart, grabbing that second folder."

Pete shook his head. "Dzekas told me to do it. He didn't say why, but you know..."

"Yeah."

Across the street, two men emerged from the liquor store. The first guy was short and thin, dressed in Arabic clothes and flip-flops, and behind him was the tall guy in the Sanitation Department uniform, and he was yelling. "What's it say on the sign? Huh? It says, 'Reserved for

Pastor.' Is your name Pastor? Huh? I don't think so. Why do I gotta roust you outa my spot every time I come here?"

The other guy stopped and turned around to yell back. "That spot is empty all day long! Why I should have to drrive all over looking for spot when that one is empty every day?"

"Because it's my spot! And how come you're selling liquor anyhow? I thought that was a sin! Ain't you guys forbidden to drink? What's Allah gonna think of that when you meet him?"

"I don't drrrink it!" the little guy yelled. "I only sell it!"

"Well that's a goddam fine distinction!" The little guy turned his back and headed for his car. "I hope the good Lord sees it your way when your day comes! I hope for your sake he doesn't just decide to roast your ass for contributing to the sorrows of all the poor bastards who come into your store every day! I hope..." But the little man had gotten into his car and slammed the door. The tall guy stomped back over to his truck and slid into the just-vacated spot. He got back out of the truck and banged the door shut, looked all around, finally spotted Cheo and Pete, who were sitting on the stoop laughing at him. The preacher looked at the ground, sucked in a big breath and shook his head.

"Only Dzekas," Cheo said. "A garbage man preacher."

"Yeah," Pete said. "Hey, why not." He fished Dzekas' ATM card out of his pocket, along with a folded sheet of hand-written directions which had a key taped to it, it was the one sheet he and Cheo had kept secret from everybody. "You hadda know Dzekas wasn't gonna listen to nobody in a fancy suit."

Cheo stood up and brushed off the seat of his jeans. "You know what? I think this guy will do it, he'll really build Dzekas his tabernacle. Let's go give the dude his money."

CHAPTER 16

City Island Pete stood up out of his crouch and watched the kid trot down to first base. The kid was eleven, and cute, which meant Mr. Generosity, Cheo's favorite umpire, shrank the strike zone to about the size of a beer can. Cheo watched Pete turn and jaw with the umpire for a moment and he wondered what they were saying, but then Pete was the kind of guy who talked to everybody. Cheo turned and walked to the back of the pitcher's mound. The Parkchester Cardinals were ahead 7-6 in the last game on their schedule, but Cheo had one more out to get, and the next kid coming up to bat looked as big as anybody he had ever pitched to. This kid was their thumper.

He glanced over at the runt who'd just drawn the walk, the kid had already started measuring out his lead at first. The kid's coach yelled at him from the sideline. Cheo was not anywhere near the pitcher's rubber, so the kid's lead didn't mean anything. Kid didn't know the rule. Still, Cheo couldn't hate the kid, in fact he envied him. Kid was eleven at the most, he had years to go. Cheo, at thirteen, knew this was his last Little League game and this year it wasn't just the long wait until next season he was facing. They had like a million kids at the public school he'd be attending next year, most of them way bigger than him, and there was no guarantee he would make their baseball team, as a matter of fact the public schools in The Bronx were so squeezed for funds there might not be a team at all. It was distinctly possible that there would be no more baseball for Cheo Hernandez, period. He eyeballed the kid at first again, who was, somewhat sheepishly, now standing right on the bag. It's okay, kid, he thought. You got plenty of time to learn... Cheo hadn't permitted himself to contemplate his own naked and empty future.

The money still didn't seem real.

His mother had talked to Pete's mother, and together the two of them had hired this red-haired Irish guy named Jerry, dude came over the apartment from Jersey, spent hours explaining the facts of life. Taxes, trusts, investments, who belonged to what, all of it fascinated the two women no end but Cheo found it so boring that after a while he just wanted to shove pencils into his eyeballs. Jerry was a bulldog, Cheo knew the guy would take care of them all but if he had to listen to much more of it his head was gonna split in half.

All the kids from both teams were yelling now, cheering and screaming and pumping fists. Cheo made his way back to the rubber and wiped the sweat out of his eyes. Pete finally quit yakking with the umpire and looked over at Coach. Coach, wearing his same old intense and constipated scowl, stared back at Pete and nodded once. Coach had some friend of his sitting next to him on the bench, except for being White the guy could have been Coach's twin, he even had the same scowl on his puss but he wasn't looking at Pete, he was watching Cheo.

Cheo toed the rubber, leaned in for the sign.

Pete held down one finger.

Fastball.

Well, yeah. What else was new.

Cheo looked at first, stepped off, and the kid dove back hastily. There was no way Cheo was gonna throw over, not now, if his first baseman missed the throw the kid would wind up on second, in scoring position...

He toed the rubber again and they went through the whole ritual all over.

Pelios had gotten his picture in the paper, they told a mostly true story about how the guy had done time to keep the love of his life out of jail. It all seemed, still, completely demented to Cheo, but then there were some guys who were funny that way. The reporter had asked Pelios if he intended on suing the city for wrongful imprisonment but Pelios had told him he preferred to let bygones be bygones, which didn't sound like Pelios at all unless you knew that Pelios had places to go and storage units to empty. Right after he'd been interviewed, Pelios had checked himself out of the hospital and dropped out of sight, now nobody knew for sure where he was. Cheo was okay with that because he didn't want to be a pirate, he wanted to be a kid, a Parkchester Cardinal, and another year of eligibility would have been nice but what could you do.

He checked the kid at first again, then he kicked and threw. It was a fastball, a good one, Cheo had been fooling with his grip and his fastball had some movement on it now, this one started out right down the middle but then ran away from the left-handed batter. The kid tried to check his swing but he couldn't, a good fastball will do that to you.

Strike one.

Cheo glanced over at Coach, who was wiping his hands on his shirt and gabbing to his buddy on the bench. It was hard to tell if Coach was still mad at him. It was tough enough when he yelled at you, but when he didn't talk to you at all it was worse, Coach was the one man in the world that Cheo cared about impressing but the guy was nearly impossible to read. Cheo caught the toss back from Pete, stuck the ball in his glove while he wiped the sweat off his face again. The noise was beginning to grow, everyone from both teams seemed to be yelling at him, either support or insult, depending on the uniform. Even a few of the parents in attendance joined in.

Unless you believed in spirits, Dzekas was dead and buried. Cheo wasn't sure where he was with that. It was a hard thing for him to wrap his head around, though, the idea that the guy had been so alive, so real and so crazy and now he was either simply gone, or maybe just out of reach somehow. That's how Cheo had come to think of it because he couldn't get with the guy not being something, somehow, somewhere.

Pete was calling for a fastball, up.

High cheese.

Smoke.

The kid at first didn't look like he was going anywhere so Cheo went into his full windup, high leg kick and all, threw a letter-high fastball that was as straight as an arrow. The kid got around on it but he swung just under the ball and it caromed straight back over the umpire's head and banged hard off the backstop. A half-inch lower, maybe, and the ball would probably be in orbit right about now. Cheo knew he'd gotten away with one but it counted as strike two anyhow.

Pete's return smacked into the webbing of his glove.

I hope I remember this when I get old, Cheo thought, like a hundred years from now I wanna remember catching that throw from Pete, I wanna remember the guy at bat, the runt standing on first, even Coach sitting over there looking like he's about to crap out a turnip. Nothing in life could ever be cooler than this, not even sliding down off the Willy B and running for daylight. There was no question that after today he would never wear the uniform of a Parkchester Cardinal again but right now this was as good as anything he could think of.

Pete held down two fingers.

He was calling for the curve.

Cheo shook him off. He didn't want to give Coach a heart attack.

Pete stared back. Held down the same two fingers.

Dude was crazy... Cheo glanced over at Coach to find the man staring back at him. Coach nodded once, looking even more irritated than usual. His unspoken message: you get to throw your curve one time so you better make it a good one...

He looked back at Pete and nodded.

The ball came out of his hand, spinning madly, for the first long, stretched out nanosecond it looked like it was gonna hit the batter right between the eyes. The kid's knees buckled, his brain seemed to forget what to do with the bat as it concentrated on getting out of the path of the ball but then the ball arced, diving and slicing away from the batter like a swallow after a dragonfly. The umpire's mouth dropped open and his eyes went wide as the ball spun earthward, bisecting the strike zone just before it smacked into Pete's motionless glove with a loud pop.

The whole world stood up and went crazy.

The kid at the plate dropped his bat and staggered backward, everybody roared as the umpire jumped up out of his crouch and pumped his fist because this time even he knew it was a strike. That's what Pete had been jawing at him about, Cheo thought, Pete must have told the guy what pitch he was gonna call and when he was gonna call it, the umpire called it a strike because Pete sold him on it first...

Cheo wanted to go get the ball but he couldn't because his infielders mobbed him and started screaming and thumping him with their gloves, the guys off the bench were next and the outfielders were coming hard to join in. The air seemed thicker than it had a moment ago, heavy with joy and triumph but Cheo could taste the sorrow too, because he'd stood on the mound for that one moment with the ball in his hand, the very embodiment of everything he had ever wanted and now it was all slipping away. The elation of winning felt like a poor and distant cousin. The eleven year old who'd been standing on first base walked over, picked up the baseball, and walked away with it.

Time swam by.

Cheo bottled up his small regret and joined the celebration as best he could because it was a team sport after all, they had all done this thing together. It seemed to him that every Cardinal, each in his own way, was trying to hold on to the moment, to capture a bit of that feeling before it broke apart and melted away. People were talking everywhere, kids reliving the game, parents congratulating Coach, and Coach's friend was talking to City Island Pete. Cheo came down out of the cloud in time to hear him say, "You know something, I didn't come here looking for a catcher but I think that line drive you hit in the fourth put a dent in the outfield fence. If your mother agrees, Sacred Heart would love to have you on our team." And then they both turned and looked at Cheo. Pete wore a smile that looked like it would break his face in half as Coach's buddy reached out and grabbed Cheo. "C'mere, kid," the guy said. "You ain't getting away from me."

It wasn't over after all.

There would be another baseball season for Cheo Hernandez.

finito